D0803884

A Christmas of Grace

By

Dr. Karen Hutchins Pirnot

This is a work of fiction. Any resemblance to living or deceased persons or to events portrayed in this publication is purely coincidental.

Copyright 2012 by Dr. Karen Hutchins Pirnot
All rights reserved

No part of this publication may be reproduced, stored in a retrieval system, transmitted in any form or by any means, electronic, mechanical, photocopying, recording or otherwise without prior written permission of the author and/or illustrator. As per the U.S. Copyright Act of 1976, using any part of this publication without the permission of the author/publisher constitutes unlawful piracy and theft of the author's intellectual property.

For information regarding permission, contact:
www.drpirnotbooks.com

ISBN-13:978-1481098168

Printed in the United States of America
Printed:

For my Children
And my Grandchildren

Always keep the spirit of Christmas
In your hearts

A special thank you to
Margaret Rutter-Todd and Virginia Dale Keith
Your suggestions and proofing diligence only makes it better.

Chapter One

"Hush up now, Henry James. I can't hear a word they're saying and I got me an idea that it's a mighty important discussion."

Henry was only momentarily irritated by his sister's orders. At nearly six years of age, Henry was used to his eleven year old sister ordering him about. In fact, more than once, her demands had spared him humiliation, pain or despair. For the most part, Henry Gillian trusted his sister Grace to act in his behalf. He remained quiet while Grace listened at the door of the tiny bedroom they shared.

"I can't help it, Lou Ann, it's Betty. She insists that you're a worthless housekeeper and she's suspicious that you and me, well, we're doing more than housekeeping."

"You flatter yourself, Barry."

"Aw, come on, Lou Ann. I know I ain't exactly a movie star, but at least, I'm trying to help out you and the little ones."

At the comment about *little ones,* Grace frowned and gritted her teeth. For as long as she could remember, Grace Gillian had pictured herself as a very mature girl. And her actions had proven her to be correct, at least most of the time.

"Barry, you know I don't have no other options. There's no one that will hire me with these kids and we got nowhere else to live."

"Sorry, Lou Ann. Betty's had enough and I guess maybe I have too. Our deal was that you clean our place for the right to stay in the trailer. And then, you told me you could manage the lot rent. You ain't paid that in four months now and we just can't afford to let it go on. If you can't come up with the lot rent by Saturday, you gotta leave."

"Just like that?"

"Just like that, Lou Ann. Its pay day Saturday or you're out of here." Grace could hear the door slam. Then, she listened for the predictable clink of ice in the glass. Five second later, the click was there and Grace knew it would be useless to try to talk with her mother yet that night. The stuff in the brown bottle on the first shelf to the right of the sink would take care of that.

Grace went back to the double bed she had shared with Henry for the past year. She stroked his head and told him to get to sleep.

"What's going on, Grace? I'm almost six now and I deserve to know what's happening."

"I know, Henry. But, right now, I need to get me in some thinking time before I drift off to sleep. You'd best get some rest now. It could be rough for us for awhile."

"Again?" Henry asked.

"Yeah, again, Henry. Sorry but that's just the way it is. Night now."

"Night, Grace. I love you to the moon."

"I love you there and back, Henry. Go to sleep now."

Henry snuggled into the covers and turned his back away from Grace. He stared out the window and watched the stars glimmer as he drifted off to sleep.

Grace lay awake until the wee hours of the morning, wondering how they would survive if they were evicted from the trailer. Saturday was only two days away.

Chapter Two

The next morning, Grace slept in until eight o'clock.

The Christmas holiday break from school had just begun and

she fully intended to catch up on some of her sleep. Lately,

Grace's mother Lou Ann had taken to bringing home strange

men at night. Whenever Grace questioned her mother about

strangers being in the house, Lou Ann would make up

excuses about them being "cousins." She said they just

needed a place to stay for the night.

Lou Ann explained that the men usually left some

money for the privilege of staying the night and Grace

shouldn't ought to complain about the inconvenience.

In truth, Grace didn't care all that much about her mother's company. But she wished they were not so noisy. Sometimes, their giggling and yelling kept her up all hours of the night and she would fall asleep in school the next day. She had tried telling her mother about how the company bothered her but lately, Lou Ann had listened less and less. She always appeared groggy and when she talked, her words were slurred.

One weekend when Lou Ann was gone for all of Saturday night, Grace checked the brown bottles that always seemed to make her mother happy. She knew it was liquor and she knew the stuff in the brown bottle was beginning to affect the family in a really bad way. More and more, Grace was taking over the care of her little brother Henry.

Grace went to the kitchen, hoping to ask her mother about the conversation she had heard the previous meeting. Her mother was nowhere in sight and there was no note. Lou Ann had disappeared from time to time in the past, sometimes for overnight. But she had always left a note for Grace. Typically, the notes would say that Lou Ann had a "quickie" cleaning job and that she would be home later with groceries. That always meant that Grace was to get Henry up and ready for school. Since there was no school today, Grace decided to just let Henry sleep. She poured some Rice Krispies for herself and poured slightly sour milk over the cereal. She sat at the small table which backed up to a bench in the tiny kitchen area of the mobile home.

Grace had always hated the mobile home. She was teased unmercifully at school about her family being "poor, white trash." In fact, the Black kids at school were now treated with more respect than was Grace. She had only one friend in her fifth grade class. Rosie Tuttle was a Black child and she didn't seem to care that Grace's family had even less than did her own family. Rosie lived two blocks from the mobile home park. Her family lived in a weathered clapboard house but Rosie and her brother Will seemed happy enough with what they had. Mr. Tuttle had a job at the canning factory and her mother worked part-time at the textile works. The Tuttles always had food on the table and Rosie always wore clean clothes. Unlike Grace's clothes, if there were tears, someone had fixed the tear in Rosie's clothes so it wasn't so noticeable.

For a moment, Grace pondered why her own mother did not seem able to hold a job. In the past few years, Lou Ann had tried working at a convenience store, the textile factory, the Tenth Street Diner, a laundromat and most recently, cleaning house for the landlord. The cleaning job had lasted longer than any of the others. At least, it enabled the Gillian family to have a roof over their heads.

Grace took another spoonful of her cereal and her mind flashed back to before she had started to school. For five years, it had been just Grace and her mother and they seemed to do just fine. For awhile, Lou Ann received monthly checks that would pretty nearly cover what they really needed. But then, the checks stopped and Lou Ann had tried her hand at a real job. There had never been a father in the picture for Grace, only a series of men who came and went. Lou Ann seemed to be able to attract about any man she wanted with her strawberry blond hair, ice-blue eyes and a figure that instantly drew men's attention to her. The problem was Lou Ann did not seem capable of keeping anyone in her life, be it man or woman. She had always told Grace that it was good for a woman to be independent. Whenever she said it lately, Grace wanted to asked her mother, "Yeah, and how is that working out for you?" But she knew it would only hurt Lou Ann, so she remained quiet, contemplating how at eleven years of age, she could possibly raise her brother.

Even though she was not a particularly great student, Grace did well enough in her fifth grade studies at Parks Elementary School in Little Rock, Arkansas. The school used to have a different name but it was renamed for Rosa Parks in 1960 when Grace started the second grade. One of the history lessons Grace had learned was how, in the late 1950's Rosa Parks refused to sit in the back of the bus like the other Black passengers. When she heard the story, Grace wanted to be just like Rosa Parks.

Grace's teacher Miss Metters seemed to understand that Grace had more than her share of responsibility at home and she didn't press her for the better grades that she knew Grace was capable of delivering. Grace liked science and that was the only class that she really put any effort into so that she could see that A on her report card.

About the time Grace started to school, Lou Ann announced that Grace was going to have a new little brother or sister. At first, Grace was excited. She had oftentimes dreamed of being in a *real* family with two parents. As long as the baby's father wasn't mean, Grace thought she could accept him. But then, Lou Ann said the baby's father would not be joining the family and Grace let that balloon dream float up to the sky and disappear from view, just like all the rest of her pipe dreams.

Although she had secretly hoped for a baby sister, Grace was happy enough with Henry James. He was a good baby as baby's go but he seemed to need ongoing attention. Even when Henry was very young, Lou Ann would go out, leaving Grace in charge of her younger brother and Grace now thought that Lou Ann's comings and goings tended to make Henry somewhat anxious.

As Grace continued to daydream, Henry entered the kitchen and asked, "What's for breakfast?"

Grace rose and went to the cupboard to get a clean bowl for her brother. She poured in a generous portion of Krispy Pops and poured milk over the cereal. Henry just loved to hear the cereal as it snapped and popped. But after the initial fun, Henry thought the cereal got soggy way too fast. He gobbled up the cereal hoping to consume it while it still had some crunch in it. When he got the last spoonful, he looked at Grace and made a face saying, "Yuk! This milk is sour, Grace! Why did you give me sour milk?"

Grace just shrugged and replied, "Just be thankful you got any at all, Henry." That was Grace's standard reply to Henry's frequent statements of dissatisfaction with the material things in life. Lately, he tended to make a face and leave it alone.

"Where's Mom?" Henry asked.

"Don't know, Henry. Maybe she's out looking for a job. Maybe she's out looking for a place to live."

"We have a place to live," Henry remarked.

"Only for another day or two, Henry. Then we have to move."

"Who says?"

"Mr. Kepler says, Henry. Mom hasn't been paying the lot fee and they won't let her work for them anymore. So..."

"Grace, we *have* to have a place to stay. I mean, it's winter, Grace; it's cold out there!" Henry began to look panicky.

Grace shook her head. She knew that December in Little Rock meant that the daytime temperatures would be lucky to reach the mid-forties. She also knew it was no time to be homeless.

Henry began to cry and when his crying reached sobbing proportion, Grace went to him and held him in her arms. "Don't do that, Henry. It doesn't make things any easier for us. Mom will think of something."

"And if she doesn't...?" Henry asked in between sobs.

"Then, I'll think of something. Now, you get yourself washed up and I'll get out some of my money and we'll walk to the store and get some fresh milk."

"Do we have enough to get a box of Wheat Flakes too, Grace?"

"Wheat Flakes? Why do we need Wheat Flakes? We have a half full box of Krispy Pops, Henry."

"'Cause, Grace, Wheat Flakes are what champions eat and I want to be a champion."

"In what?" Grace asked, amused by her little brother's wish list.

"Pretty much anything, I think," Henry replied.

"I guess I know what you mean, Henry. Let me go check." Grace went to the bedroom and took out the envelope she had hidden between the mattress and the box springs. Lately, she was having to dip into her savings as Lou Ann spent more and more money on the brown bottles that made her go to sleep.

Grace counted out the bills and the change. It added up to eight dollars and thirty-two cents. A gallon of milk would be $1.06. If she got only a half-gallon or maybe, even a quart of milk, she might be able to squeeze in a small box of Wheat Flakes and still stay under a dollar. Grace made it a rule to never spend more than a dollar for groceries. It was just too much to spend it on things you really didn't need. The little money she earned from doing chores for neighbors was fast being used for food.

When Grace went back to the kitchen, Henry was putting the dirty bowls in the sink. Grace told him to go clean up and to be sure to wear his heavier jacket for the walk to the store. She checked the food cupboard and found six slices of white bread and about a third of a jar of peanut butter. There was an apple in the refrigerator. She had dinner covered that night. Because they had eaten a later breakfast, they would probably skip lunch.

Henry came out of the bathroom fifteen minutes later and went to their room to put on his play clothes. Grace washed out the breakfast dishes along with two glasses her mother had used the previous evening. Lately, Lou Ann did not seem interested in food.

Grace went back into the bedroom and smoothed out the covers on the bed she shared with Henry. Henry was just finishing zipping up his well-worn blue jeans.

"Can we go to a movie today, Grace?" he asked with a hopeful look in his captivating green eyes. Grace tussled his blond head of hair and said, "Not today, son." She oftentimes referred to Henry that way, especially when she wanted to appear older and in charge of things.

The children put on their jackets and Grace then stuck her own stocking cap on Henry's head. "We'll just put our hands in our pockets if they get cold," she suggested, anticipating some whining from Henry about being cold and not having mittens.

Grace felt for the dollar and twenty-five cents in her pants pocket. At the last minute, she had stuck in an extra quarter *just in case*. For as long as she could remember, Grace had always had a *just in case* backup plan for when something went wrong. She really hated being caught unaware. By planning ahead, she could always remain calm. She hated that her little brother always seemed anxious and afraid of what might be just around the corner.

"Shall we stop in and say hi to Rosie, Grace?" Henry asked as the two approached the Tuttle home.

"Nope, she isn't there, Henry. They all went to Mississippi to Rosie's grandmother's house for the holidays."

"How can they do that, Grace? Doesn't it cost a lot of money?"

"Sure it does, Henry. But Mr. and Mrs. Tuttle both get paid vacations from their work and they take it now instead of in the summer."

"They get paid for not working?" Henry asked with disbelief.

"Yup! That's what happens when you have a regular job, Henry. They reward you for your hard work by giving you time off."

"Man, has Mom ever gotten paid time off, Grace?" Henry asked with wide eyes.

"Never, Henry, never. But, I'm gonna get it when I go to work. And you better think about it too if you're smart."

"I will, Grace," Henry said with a resolute expression on his face. "I'm gonna make so much money that I won't know what to do with it, that's what I'm gonna do, Grace. Just you watch."

As they approached Rucker's Family Grocery, Grace smiled and placed her hand on Henry's shoulder. It was her signal to remind her brother that stores expected good conduct from children.

The mobile home park was only a couple of blocks from 9th Street West, an area that was predominantly a Black and poor White population. There were small, family owned stores there and local residents could pretty much stay in the area and not have to travel to Main Street where the larger department stores were. On Main Street, Blacks still risked rejection. Grace liked the small, community stores and she stayed pretty much in the area for any purchases she might make for the family.

As the children went into the grocery store, the bell on the door rang and Mrs. Rucker said, "Oh there they are, my precious little Gillians. I swear Grace, you grow an inch taller every day I see you!"

That was Mrs. Rucker's standard greeting. Grace just smiled and headed to the cooler. She took out a quart of milk and took it to the counter while Henry looked around.

"Only a quart today?" Mrs. Rucker asked. "Most generally, you youngsters come in for a gallon."

"Well," Grace said tentatively, trying to think of the right way to respond. "We might be going away for the holidays so we'd best not stock up too much so's things spoil," she said in a somewhat convincing manner.

Henry came running to the counter with a giant box of Wheat Flakes and Grace asked Mrs. Rucker if they had a smaller box. Mrs. Rucker went back to the rows of dry goods and came back with a box about two thirds the size of the one Henry had picked out. She added up the milk and the cereal on an invoice form. The grocery story had still not gone to the fancy adding machines that the larger stores were using.

"That'll be one dollar and three cents, little missy," Mrs. Rucker said with a smile.

Grace pulled out the dollar bill and the quarter and laid it on the counter as Henry ogled the glass jar filled with candy canes. Grace was just about to ask the price of the candy canes when Mrs. Rucker opened the jar, reached in and pulled out two candies.

"Being the holidays and all, consider it a gift," she said as she winked at Grace. Mrs. Rucker went to the ancient cash register and put in the dollar bill. Then, she went back to the counter and handed back the quarter to Grace saying the government surely didn't need her three cents as much as her family did. Grace smiled and thanked her.   As the children exited the store, Mrs. Rucker called out, "I hope you have a wonderful holiday wherever you're going kids!"

"Are we going somewhere for the holiday's, Grace?" Henry asked with confusion and anticipation fighting for a place on his expressive face.

"It sorta looks that way, son," Grace replied as she stuck her candy cane in her jacket pocket. "Save yours too, Henry," she added.

Chapter Three

The children walked quickly back to the house and deposited the milk in the refrigerator. Grace put the Wheat Flakes in the food cupboard while Henry held his crotch and raced off to the bathroom. Cold weather had always had that effect on Henry.

Grace looked around, hoping to find her mother splayed out on her bed at the other end of the trailer. She was nowhere around. Grace hoped she would not be gone for another "overnight" while their living arrangements were so much up in the air. She wished they had a place to go like other families. Lou Ann was an only child and her parents were both dead. Grace knew of no family members because she had no idea of who her own father or Henry's father was.

The only thing she could think to do was to somehow entertain Henry to keep his mind off things in general.

When Henry came out of the bathroom, Grace asked, "How about we do some window shopping, Henry?"

"What's that?"

"It's when you don't plan to spend any money and you just go up and down the streets looking in the windows. It's just for fun, Henry."

When Henry looked a bit dubious, Grace added, "The big stores on Main Street will be all decorated for Christmas, Henry. It should be really pretty."

"Could we look at some model cars and maybe a train, Grace?"

"I don't know why not, son. Let's get going then," Grace ordered with a smile. She helped Henry zip up his jacket and put the stocking cap back on him. This was one time Grace was grateful for the thick, lush head of auburn hair she must have inherited from her father. Her shoulder-length hair provided some measure of protection to her head as the December winds kicked up from time to time.

It was eight blocks to the downtown district from the Razorback Trailer Park at Gaines Street and 6th Street West. Grace momentarily considered paying for the bus. It would cost her ten cents but Henry could get a free ride, being only five. But then, she thought better of the plan. She wanted to save everything she had for, well, for whatever might come her way.

They walked down Gaines to 7th Street West and passed the library. Grace thought the elegant building looked like pictures of buildings she had seen in Washington D.C. She had gone into the library only once since moving to the mobile home park. That was a month ago when she had a science project to research for school. Grace thought the inside of the library was just as beautiful as the outside, with one stack of books after another. She had watched the librarians and thought how wonderful it must be to work in a place with so much knowledge. The sign on the outside of the building said: Little Rock Carnegie Library. She didn't know how a Carnegie library differed from any other library but maybe someday, she would find out.

Grace walked on the street side of the sidewalk to shield Henry from the gusts of wind and the passing traffic. When they got within a block of the main district of stores on Main Street, Henry yelled out, "Look Grace! I see some lights! I hear some music!"

One of the things Grace loved about her brother was that the smallest pleasures made him happy. They began the walk up the right side of the street, looking in at the brightly decorated window displays. At Hobby Heaven, Henry asked if they might go inside and "window shop." The children were both cold so Grace obliged. The warmth of the store was a blessing. Henry had pointed at so many toys outside that his little hands were red and chapped looking.

A clerk came up to the children and asked if they were looking for something in particular. When Grace told them they were just "browsing," the clerk scowled and told them they were welcome to look but "You mustn't touch the merchandise."

Grace laughed to herself. What kind of a word was mustn't anyway! She followed Henry around the store while he looked at one model kit after another. The prices were marked on the front of each package and after awhile, Henry looked at Grace and said, "They cost an awful lot of money, don't they, Grace?"

Grace shook her head and urged Henry around the aisle and up towards the front door. When they opened the door, Grace smiled at the clerk who was watching them with an eagle eye. "Thank you for letting us browse, sir. We saw quite a few things to tell Santa about."

Grace's remark did not pass by Henry's ears. "Are we really going to see Santa, Grace?"

Grace moaned and thought for a moment. "He's really busy now, Henry. If we happen to run into him, we'll say our hellos, okay?" Henry smiled, content to leave it at that for now.

It was getting close to midafternoon and Henry said he was hungry. Grace suggested they cross the street and sit on a bench on the other side. There was no wind and it was warmer. Grace told Henry they could both have their candy cane treats now and that would hold them over until dinner.

The children took their seats and carefully unwrapped their candy canes. Neither child wanted to break the stalk of the cane. That treat was best eaten in the whole, sucking on the stem as you held the handle firmly in your hand. It took a full twenty minutes for the children to chew on the last of the curved handle and both were beginning to shiver by then.

Grace looked up the street and then smiled. "Look, Henry, Macy's is just up the street there! We can ride the escalators and look at the lights and stuff. How about it?"

Henry began to run ahead and Grace had to run to catch up with him. When they both got to the main display windows, Henry said "Wow Grace, look at that train! It's going all around the tree!"

Grace took Henry's hand and led him inside the store. They both sighed at the warmth and they unzipped their coats. Henry said he had never seen so many lights and Grace simply took in the warmth and the smells coming from the cosmetics counters. They had perfume displays on the counters and women were sampling the sprays. Grace wanted to do that herself, but she didn't want to draw attention to herself or Henry.

A clerk approached the children with a smile and asked if they were alone. Grace nudged Henry on his left shoulder and he knew it was the signal to "shut up." Grace explained to the clerk that their mother was doing a bit of shopping and she was to take her little brother to the Winter Wonderland display.

"Oh, well, that's upstairs, child. You'll need to take the escalator or perhaps the elevator."

As Grace thanked the clerk, Henry got a mischievous smile on his face and said, "Or maybe both, huh, Grace?"

Grace had Henry stand in front of her as he made his way onto the escalator. He wanted to walk up the steps but Grace cautioned him it would be unsafe. He contented himself by staring at his image in the mirrors that covered the walls adjacent to the escalator. Henry made faces at his own image and Grace had to control herself so as not to burst out laughing.

When they reached the top of the escalator, Grace leaned down to Henry and said, "Now no running, son. We don't want to attract any attention and we for sure do NOT want to get into trouble with any adults. Henry looked placid and took his sister's hand. They could hear the tune *Toyland* playing in the distance so they both followed the sound until a winter wonderland appeared directly in front of them.

There appeared to be about a dozen Christmas trees, all frosted white and placed in a circle. In between the trees were wrapped presents and toys which appeared about to be wrapped. A small Santa's workshop had been set up to the left. The children gravitated toward that area. Another train similar to the one in the window was running in a small circle, with houses and stores placed on the outside. Everything was covered in snow.

"It's fake, I know it is, right, Grace?" Henry asked as he reached out to touch the snow fields.

Grace grabbed Henry's hand and said, "Yes, it's fake, Henry. It's just a display and we aren't allowed to touch it." Henry put the potentially offending hand in his jacket pocket.

They walked all around the workshop and Henry said he'd like to have about everything on display. "Not the dolls, though," he quickly added. As they approached the end of the workshop display, they appeared directly in front of a roped-off area in which an authentic-looking Santa sat, talking with children who waited in line.

"Oh, please, Grace, can't I talk with him, please, Grace," Henry begged.

"I don't know, Henry, he looks pretty busy with those other kids." Grace didn't want Henry to get his hopes up about some Christmas toy he would probably never get. The priority right now seemed to be getting a place to stay. But then, Grace thought to herself, "Well, what could it hurt? He's just a kid and he's gotta believe in something."

"Okay, then, let's get in line." They were in no hurry to get back to a house that would no longer be theirs in another day.

As the children made their way up the line, there was Christmas music being played and their spirits began to lift. "Look, Grace. Santa is giving away something." Henry studied the sacks being handed to the children who sat on Santa's lap. "I wonder what it is, Grace."

Grace just shrugged. She guessed that something was better than nothing. So, they stayed in line and moved closer and closer to Santa.

Finally, it was Henry's turn and he literally ran to Santa and jumped in the lap of the jovial and good-hearted man. "Well, well, who do we have here?" Santa asked as Henry looked at the old man expectantly.

"I'm Henry, sir, Henry James Gillian."

"Oh, why yes, of course, it's Henry James! Why, you've grown so much since last year, I hardly recognized you!" Santa bellowed out. Grace had to laugh at that one. Santa certainly knew how to cover himself!

Grace patiently waited while Santa asked Henry the usual questions about whether he had been a good boy and had helped out his mom and dad. Henry replied factually that he had no dad that he knew about but that he had been trying to help out his mother. Henry told Santa he wanted a model car for Christmas. Santa asked if there was a particular one Henry had his mind set on and Henry replied that anyone would probably do but that he really liked the '57 Chevy. Santa thanked Henry for visiting him and he eased the boy off his lap as an elf came up to give a sack to Henry. As Henry turned to leave, he yelled, "And don't forget the glue, Santa!"

Grace began to move toward Henry when the elf pushed her toward Santa. "You're never too old to visit with Santa, little girl," he said. Grace was furious about being called a little girl but fortunately, Santa seemed to notice her discomfort. He motioned her over with the index finger of his right hand. Curious as to what he wanted, Grace took the bait and went to Santa.

"I'm not sitting on anyone's lap no matter who they are," Grace said directly. Santa grinned and then asked her if their father had recently died.

"I really couldn't say, Santa. He's just never been a factor in our lives."

"Well then, anything you can think of for Santa to bring you then, Grace?" Santa asked.

Grace was flabbergasted! How did Santa know her name? And then, she reasoned that the old man must have heard Henry refer to her. She thought for just a moment and leaned in toward Santa's left ear. "We could use a place to live if you have anything like that."

Grace then stood straight up, winked at Santa and made her way down the ramp to where Henry was waiting. An elf handed her a sack just like the one Henry had received and Grace took it without hesitation. She looked back at Santa who still appeared to have a puzzled look on his face.

"Can we open our sacks now, Grace?" Henry asked excitedly.

"Let's go sit on those benches and take a load off," Grace suggested. "Then, we can have a look-see."

Henry followed his sister to an unoccupied bench and began to open his sack, being careful not to tear the paper. It was stapled together, with a curly red and green ribbon hanging from the staple. Below the ribbon was a sticker picture of a child sitting on Santa's lap. Grace thought that someone had gone to a lot of trouble making up the sacks.

"Wow! Look at all the stuff in here, Grace!" Henry said in amazement. "There's a chocolate bar and a candy cane and…, oh, it's a new toothbrush! I guess you need the toothbrush after eating all the candy, huh, Grace?"

"I guess so, Henry. I got a coloring book in mine and a package of four crayons too. Did you get that?"

Henry nodded his head as he continued to search his sack. "Lookee here, Grace! There's a ring on the bottom! I bet it's a magic ring, don't you think?"

Grace initially shook her head and then, not wanting to ruin her brother's hopes and dreams, she replied, "It could be, son. You never know about those things. Shall we put them on and make a wish?"

"Right here?" Henry asked.

"Good a place as any," Grace replied.

Grace tried the ring on all her fingers and finally, placed it on her left pinkie. Henry also tried the ring on his fingers and his ring ended up on his right thumb. "Okay," Grace instructed, "if I remember this magic ring thing right, you have to close your eyes and make a wish. Then, we open our eyes and hit our rings together to seal the deal. Ready?"

Henry nodded and closed his eyes. His eyes remained closed long after Grace had made her wish and opened her eyes. She waited and finally, Henry's eyes fluttered and then opened. They held right hand to left hand and clinked their rings together. Grace was amazed that the fake stones even stayed in the setting.

"Wanna know what I wished for, Grace?" Henry asked.

"Nope, it won't come true if you tell anyone, Henry." Grace wanted to add that it wouldn't come true anyway but she was not about to be the spoilsport when Henry was in such a good mood. He hadn't been anxious all afternoon. Grace took a deep breath and hoped that Lou Ann would be home when they got back from their window shopping expedition. If not, Henry's anxiety would begin.

"Tell you what, Henry, let's make a pit stop at the bathrooms before we head on home."

Henry remained silent. Finally, Grace asked, "What now?"

Henry looked to his right and asked, "I was wondering if we could maybe watch those tv stations, Grace." He looked at Grace's sullen expression and added, "Only for a few minutes."

Grace sighed. How could she deprive her brother of a few more minutes of pleasure? They were probably the only family in school without a television set. "Okay, but first, the bathrooms, Henry."

Grace took Henry's hand and led him to the women's restroom. "I can go in the boy's, Grace," Henry pleaded.

But, Grace would have none of that. She had heard about children being taken away in just such circumstances and she was not about to lose the only brother she had.

Fortunately, there was only one lady in the women's restroom and she paid no attention to the children. Grace pointed to one stall and she took the one right next to it. When Henry came out, Grace checked his zipper to see that it was closed and then instructed her brother to wash his hands. "Use soap," she instructed.

Henry loved the soap in restrooms. He used five times more than he needed and Grace had a terrible time trying to wash off all the soap before she could dry Henry's hands.

Both children felt refreshed as they headed to the television department where six TVs' were simultaneously playing. For almost an hour, the children went from one set to the next and then, back again. They saw an advertisement for a performance from the English group the Beatles. Henry thought it was a stupid name. Grace had heard of the group from girls at school but she had not yet heard the Beatles sing. "They were on the Jack Paar Show, Henry. That's a show that plays really late at night, so we're not likely to catch them."

"Look at this one, Grace. It has monsters in it. They live in a really weird house too. The children watched for several minutes until the announcer said that the Addams Family would be on again after the break. Another set had a show on called Gomer Pyle and Henry thought the guy talked really funny. Grace went to a set that was showing an episode of Gilligan's Island and she thought she might like to be stranded. The people on the show seemed to be getting on just fine.

"These sure are some good shows, huh, Grace?" Henry asked.

"I guess, if you're into that kind of thing I mean. Personally, I think it's better to read and then imagine the things you're reading about."

"You have to have books for that, Grace. And besides, I can't read yet," Henry said with a bit of a pouty face.

"Well maybe we'll just have to do something about that, son," Grace said directly. "Now, it's about time we head on home."

"Could I eat a candy on the way, Grace? My tummy is beginning to growl for something."

"Tell you what, when we get outside the store, we'll each break off four squares of the Hershey bar. We'll eat those four pieces and save the rest for later. Deal?" she asked.

Henry reasoned that something was better than nothing and he agreed. On the way out of the store, the same clerk who had greeted the children came up to them and said,

"My word, don't tell me you two have been alone all this time!"

Henry looked at Grace and his eyes gave confirmation that he would not say a word. "Oh, heavens no," Grace said in a highly convincing voice. "Mom just went out to get the car warmed up. We're meeting her out front," and they raced on through the set of revolving doors.

When they got to the corner, Grace stopped and true to her word, she helped Henry carefully unwrap the Hershey bar. She broke off four squares and handed them to him. While Grace got out her own candy bar, Henry meticulously broke off half of the square and then broke it into four pieces. "Ummm," he said as the chocolate hit his taste buds.

They walked quickly and were home within twenty minutes. As they approached the front door, Grace said a silent prayer that her mother would be there. They entered the house and Grace did a quick reconnaissance of the house only to discover that Santa had let her down again.

Chapter Four

That night, the children had peanut butter sandwiches, half an apple apiece and another four squares of their Hershey bar. Grace poured them both half a glass of milk, saving some for their breakfast cereal in the morning.

Grace made Henry take a shower and she washed his hair. She tucked him in and said he should "sleep tight." Henry said he would rather "sleep loose" because it was more comfortable and Grace told him to spread out then. "If you're all over the bed when I come in, I'll just shove you off the bed, so enjoy it while you can, son!"

Henry reached up and pulled at Grace's neck so she had to get close to his face. "I'm so glad you don't leave like Mom does, Grace. I feel safe when you're here." He kissed

Grace's forehead and she kissed him back. "I love you to the moon, Grace."

"And I love you to the moon and back, Henry." Grace tucked in her little brother and he again turned toward the window where he gazed out at the stars.

Grace checked around the house, looking for any clues as to the whereabouts of her mother. She thought about going to the bar on 9th Street West but did not want to leave Henry alone. She could not imagine what her mother could be thinking and she could not figure out what to do in case her mother failed to return in the morning to pay the lot fee.

It was eleven o'clock before Grace went to bed. She ruminated through the night, trying to come up with some way to keep a roof over her head if Lou Ann failed to show. Generally if Lou Ann went out for the night, she would only be gone for one night. However, in the past two months Lou Ann had stayed out for two nights on two separate occasions and Grace had no idea where her mother had been. If Lou

Ann was drinking, she was highly unpredictable and lately, Lou Ann had been drinking more and more.

Grace finally fell asleep around four in the morning. By then, she had figured out a rough plan of how to keep Henry and herself safe, if only for a couple of days.

The children both slept in until nine o'clock the next morning. Grace awoke to Henry poking her on the shoulder. "Why is it so cold in here, Grace?" he asked.

Grace sat up and rubbed her eyes. She put the blanket down to her waist and was immediately cold. When she talked, she could see her breath. She immediately understood that the electricity had been turned off.

Chapter Five

Urging Henry to dress as quickly as he could, Grace went to the kitchen. She opened the refrigerator to find the milk barely cool. It was colder in the trailer than it was in the refrigerator. The electricity must have been turned off at midnight.

She got out the cereal bowls and placed the milk on the table. When Henry came in, Grace told him there was no electricity so she couldn't make toast with the last three slices of bread. Instead, the children ate the bread mostly plain, with just a dab of peanut butter that Grace managed to scrape out of the bottom and sides of the jar.

When they were finished eating, Grace took the bowls and spoons to the sink to wash them. There was no water. She knew they were in trouble and she would have to put her plan to work.

Grace told Henry to drink up all the milk in the carton. He looked at her with a quizzical expression and she said, "Yeah, go ahead and drink it right from the carton like a slob!"

Henry did just that, dribbling a small amount down his chin and giggling as he drank.

"Henry, there's something we need to plan together and I really need your help." Grace turned and looked directly at her brother and she then went to the table and sat next to him.

Henry looked puzzled rather than alarmed so Grace decided to continue. "I'm not sure when Mom is coming back. I guess she has her own things to figure out. But it's pretty clear to me that we can't stay here now. There is no electric and there is no water. It's not a safe place to be. Do you agree with me, Henry?"

Henry nodded. He looked more concerned than anxious. Grace figured Henry needed more information before he could show his true feelings.

We don't really know anyone but Rosie's family and they're gone for awhile, right?"

Henry again nodded his head in understanding.

"So, I figure we need to stake out a place for ourselves. It has to be a place where people come and go so's we won't be noticed so much. We don't want to call attention to ourselves. Do you know why, Henry?"

This time, Henry shook his head in a manner that suggested a "no" answer.

"Well, if people think we don't have a parent to watch out over us, they'll call Children's Services and we'll be put somewhere until they find Lou Ann. They could even try to separate us, Henry."

At the last statement, Henry gave a look of panic and fear.

Immediately, Grace said, "So we have to make sure that won't happen, son, and I know just how to make sure you and I stick together, okay?"

Henry relaxed just a bit and asked, "How, Grace? How can we be sure to stay together? Where will we go?"

"We're going to stay at a place that is really part ours, Henry. It's a public place that is warm and safe and we'll just sorta extend our privileges there for awhile. We'll stay for as long as we can, I guess."

"I don't know a place like that, Grace."

"Well I do, son, and that's the important thing. But, first of all, we have to prepare for our adventure. You never go on an adventure unprepared, right?"

"I guess so but I don't know how you do that prepared thing, Grace."

"I'm really good at that, Henry. I've had to do it a lot and I can make good plans for the both of us. But you have to do something really, really important too."

"What's that, Grace?"

"You have to trust me, Henry. You have to do what I say and you have to act the really important role I give to you. Otherwise, the adventure just won't come out the way we want it to."

"How do we want it to come out, Grace?"

"We want it to come out that we are safe and happy and most of all, that we are together."

"I like that ending, Grace. I'll do my part, I promise. I can do it now 'cause I'm almost six."

"I know, Henry. You're almost grown like me. And, I'm counting on you being a big boy now so that we can have the best adventure ever!"

"It's a deal, Grace! We're partners, aren't we?" Henry asked with a great deal of enthusiasm.

"That we are, little brother. We're partners and this will be our grandest adventure. Now, we need to get prepared."

"How do we do that, Grace?"

"Glad you asked, partner! We are each going to pack up our backpacks with everything we will need. Don't take silly stuff, Henry. We need to get everything in our packs that we'll need for the next few days. We might not be able to come back to get anything, so let's be sure we get everything we'll need."

"Can I take Buster?"

Grace winced for a moment and then smiled and said, "Of course, Henry. Buster Bear has been with us all your life and I think he would want to go on our adventure. Now, I want you to pack some underwear and socks and two pair of jeans and two tee shirts. Put in your sweatshirt and a pair of pajamas and your toothbrush, of course."

Henry immediately ran to the bedroom and began to pack his clothes in his backpack while Grace thought of extra things she might want to take from the trailer. Henry was back in the kitchen in five minutes. Grace was searching through the dry goods and the refrigerator. There was nothing she could take.

Grace examined Henry's backpack and packed down the items Henry had included. Then she asked him to stuff in the cotton blanket from their bed. He asked if he could take his battered old red Tonka truck and Grace looked at him sadly as she said, "Afraid not, son. There's just no room for it. But where we're going, there will be things to do."

Grace retrieved her backpack from the hook on the bedroom wall. She packed her own clothes and got her toothbrush from the bathroom. Then, she went to her mother's bedroom and took the cotton blanket from Lou Ann's bed. She stuffed it in her backpack. She went back to the kitchen and paused for a moment. Then, she opened a drawer and took out a well-worn pack of cards and tossed them in the small zippered compartment of her backpack. Then, she got a used but still useable candle and a book of matches. In another drawer, she took out a flashlight. She got an extra set of batteries and placed everything in her backpack. Lastly, she got the envelope from under the mattress in the bedroom she and Henry shared. She put one dollar in her jeans pocket and another dollar in a zippered pocket of her jacket. The rest, she left in the envelope and she carefully shoved it into the bottom of her backpack.

"Are we ready for our adventure, Grace?" Henry asked with anticipation.

Grace put her stocking cap on Henry's head and said, "Looks like it to me, Henry. Now, it's a bit nippy out there but not too bad. Remember we have pockets for our hands and we want to try to stay warm while we walk to a very magical place.

Henry went out the door first. Grace looked around

one last time and shook her head. Then, she closed the door

and took Henry's hand and they headed down the street.

Chapter Six

They had gone only half a block when Henry asked where they were going for their adventure.

"Weee…," said Grace in an exaggerated manner, "are going to the Little Rock Carnegie Library, partner!"

Henry frowned and then said, "But we got a library in our school, Grace. Why don't we just go there?"

"School is closed now, remember? Besides, this library is much, much bigger than the one at school. It's so big that we can have one adventure after another."

"How can you have an adventure in a library?" Henry asked with skepticism in his voice. "Besides, I thought you had to be quiet in a library and you can't have an adventure and be quiet at the same time so there! You don't know everything, Grace!"

Grace took a breath before she answered. She didn't know if Henry was angry that he wasn't truly a partner in planning the adventure or if his seeming anger was masking the anxiety she hoped to avoid.

"You're right, partner. We do have to be quiet in the library." Henry stuck up his head in apparent victory.

"But, it's because we have to be quiet that we will be able to have our grand adventure. Don't you see, Henry, if everyone has to be quiet, they can't be asking us a lot of questions about why we are there so much."

"Why will we be there so much then?"

"Because, Henry, that's where we are going to stay."

"I thought you said we were going to a place that was part ours, Grace. The library isn't ours at all."

"Hmmm, you might not think so right off, Henry, but it is a public library and we are part of the public?"

"We are?"

"We are, son. The public is everybody that lives in the town."

"What part of the public are we, Grace?"

"You could say we are a small part, Henry, but we *are* part of the public."

'What part of the library do we own then, Grace?"

"Well, that's a little tougher to figure out, Henry. I think we'll look around and see what suits us and then, that part will be ours. How's that for a plan?"

"Is the library open all night, Grace?"

"No, Henry, it closes at five in the afternoon. And then, that's when part of our adventure takes place."

"You mean we have to leave and go somewhere else?"

"Well, sorta. But only to another part of the library, Henry."

"Do we own some of that part too?"

"You could say that. It's one of the more interesting parts of the library, if you want my opinion."

"I guess I do then. How do you know about all these library parts anyway, Grace?"

I was there a couple of months ago, Henry. I had to do some work for school and I spent most of the day in the library."

"Tell me about the parts, Grace."

"Well, when you first get to the front, it looks like a huge building. It has columns in front and steps leading up to the double doors in the front. You can see lots of windows.

When you go in, there is sort of a hallway and then you go into a huge room. There is a long desk where the librarian sits just to the left. If you need help, you can ask her to find a book for you. If you walk a little farther, you come to a restroom. There are two doors there. One says restroom and another says Exit."

"Like the sign in our school?"

"Yeah, the same kind of sign."

"So, you can go out the library by that door then?"

"No, that door actually leads to the steps to go downstairs. I found it accidentally when I went in the wrong door. I wondered what was down there, so I just kept going."

"Did you get in trouble for going in that door, Grace?"

"No, not really. It's part of the library too, Henry. It just isn't used much."

"What's down there?"

Mostly, it's just one great big room. There is this huge boiler that heats the library. It has lots of pipes coming out of it like it has a dozen hands sticking out or something."

"That sounds kinda scary, Grace."

"It's not really, Henry. It's mostly funny-looking. It looks kinda like a cartoon octopus. And then, there are huge book stacks down there where I guess they store the books that most people don't want to check out anymore."

"You mean they just put the books in stacks on the floor?"

"No, they put them on shelves, Henry. There must be close to a hundred shelves down there and it's nice and cozy and warm. It keeps the books from getting all damp and moldy. I saw a sign down there that says they use it for a shelter if there is a tornado or something bad like that."

"Is there a kitchen down there so you can make food, Grace?"

"No, we won't be cooking food, Henry. We will go out for our food. There are about a hundred cots there though. They are all rolled up to save room but we can each have one for ourselves. We can sleep in between the book stacks and no one will even know we are there."

"Is there a bathroom down there?"

"Hmm, I think I remember seeing a small room with a deep sink and a toilet. The janitor keeps all his cleaning supplies in there."

"Will he be there, Grace?"

"He cleans up Monday through Friday, Henry. So he won't be there over the weekend. But, he will be back on Monday and we'll have to be careful then."

"Will there be light down there, Grace?"

"There are lights, Henry, but we probably won't turn them on. I have a candle and I brought a flashlight with me. We won't need much light. Mostly, we'll just be talking and stuff."

Henry thought for some time as they continued to walk. He was looking a bit skeptical when he asked, "I thought you said this was going to be a great adventure, Grace. Where is the adventure part?"

"I was saving that for last, Henry. I'm going to teach you how to read! Then, you'll be ahead of everyone when you start first grade and you can read books all by yourself!"

"I know my letters already, Grace!" Henry said proudly.

"I know you do! That's why I know you're ready to begin to read. But you gotta promise me something, Henry."

Henry nodded and Grace continued. "You have to let me do the talking. You have to pretend you're kinda shy and that you don't like to talk to strangers."

"I don't like to talk to strangers, Grace. For real," Henry added.

"Then, I picked the perfect person to play that role in our adventure, Henry! You will be SO convincing!"

"Won't people wanna know why there's not a grown-up with us, Grace?"

"I think I have that part covered, Henry. I don't think the librarian knows us, at least not the librarian in the children's department."

"You didn't tell me about that, Grace."

"Oh, yeah, well, back past the restroom, there's a small part where all the books are for children. The tables and chairs are smaller and there is a little desk where you can ask for help from a different librarian. Mostly, she just walks around and does librarian things but she's supposed to be there if kids have questions too."

"What if she asks us why we're there so much?"

"Good question, partner! That's where you come in. Your role is very important, Henry. I will tell her that we are staying with our grandma over the holidays and that my job is to teach you how to read. Your grand adventure will be that you really *will* learn how to read and my adventure is that I get to be your teacher!"

"Will she believe you, Grace?"

"Not only will she believe me, I think she'll eat it up, Henry!"

"She'll eat what up?"

"That's just an expression, Henry, a figure of speech. It means that she will believe us because she values reading and that is what I will be teaching."

"Then why didn't ya just say that, Grace?"

"You're right, Henry. I should have just said it.

The children stopped right in front of the library and Henry commented on how big the building was. "It looks like a very important place, Grace."

"Someday, Henry, maybe we'll know just how important it is," Grace said. "Now, let's go in and scout out the place."

"Like explorers?"

"Exactly, Henry! You and I are explorers and we are just about to start our grand adventure!"

Chapter Seven

The children walked up the steps of the library and Grace pulled open the large door to the right. Henry's eyes immediately got very wide.

"I told you it was big, Henry," Grace said with a smile. Henry looked around as if he was at a circus and he instinctively stuck out his hand for Grace to hold.

Grace led them both through the large great room containing reference and adult books. When they passed the restrooms, Grace pointed to her left and Henry acknowledged that he had seen the sign. He then pointed to the other door which said EXIT to ARCHIVES and Grace whispered that was the door which led downstairs. Henry smiled, content to wait to see the basement until Grace deemed it the proper time.

They entered the children's area and a woman half-smiled at them. She had a rather stern facial expression and Henry immediately turned away and began to scan the rows and rows of books. "This is bigger than the school library alright, Grace."

Grace pointed to a table and then told Henry to take off his jacket and hang it over the back of the chair. She did the same with her jacket and then pointed to a place under the table where Henry should put his backpack. As Grace got her backpack secure underneath the table, the librarian came back into the room and headed toward the table where Grace and Henry had staked out a spot. Grace took a deep breath and smiled.

"Hello there. I'm Talia Jefferson, the children's librarian," the lady said. She was tall, probably about five feet and eight inches by Grace's best guess. She had short brown hair and deep brown eyes housed in a face which did not quickly reveal inner feelings. "May I help you find anything?" she asked.

Grace smiled and said," I'm Grace and this is my little brother Henry. We're here visiting our Nana for the holidays and I figured since there's not a lot to do at Nana's house, it would be a good time to teach my brother how to read. He'll be going into first grade soon and Mom and I would like to give him a head start.

The librarian smiled and she said, "What a wonderful idea, Grace! And Henry, you're such a lucky little boy." Henry turned his head away and acted the shy one very effectively.

The librarian turned back to Grace and said, "He's a bit the shy one, I see. Not to worry. I'll not bother you with your important mission, Grace. I think the primers you'll want to start with are all on the shelves marked A and B. I'd start with the A rack first. It has a lot of the Dick and Jane series and also the Alice and Jerry Readers."

"Oh, thank you Miss Jefferson," Grace replied. I remember those from when I first started to read. They'll be just perfect!"

The librarian smiled at Henry and he again turned away his head. He then rose and went to join Grace in looking for the reading books. In shelving row A, Grace found the Dick and Jane series. She pulled out three books as she told Henry, "These readers are kind of a *see and say* way of reading, Henry. They have great pictures that give you clues about the words below. And the words repeat a lot so's you can get of idea of what it looks like."

"Can we do the one with the dog first, Grace?" It was one of the pre-primers and would be a good first reader.

"Sure we can, Henry. That's a great choice! The dog's name is spot and he belongs to Dick and Jane."

"I wish we had a dog, Grace. I'd take really good care of him if we had a dog,"

"I know you would, Henry. Let's sit down now and I'll show you how it works. Do you know how the letters sound yet?"

"Yeah, I think so. You mean like an S sounds like ssssss…and a B sounds like Bah, Bah. Is that what you mean?"

"It's exactly what I mean, son. That makes it easier to learn the words. Now, look at this first picture. Tell me what you see."

"I see Dick and Jane watching the dog Spot."

"Good, now what is Spot doing?"

"He's running away from them."

"Right again! You're good at this, Henry. Now, look at this word at the top of the page and see if you can sound out the word."

Henry started to growl as he sounded out the letter R. He tried to sound out the U but had no luck. Grace explained that sometimes, two letters sort of went together. She told him the U and the N together sounded like UN.

Henry frowned and then said, "I got it Grace! The R and the UN together make up run, is that it?"

"You got it, son! And see, the picture sort of tells the story below. I'm going to point out the words as I go along. I will read the first two lines and then, you see if you can read the last line. Grace read the simple sentence about Jane and then the next sentence about Dick. "Your turn now, Henry."

Henry studied the three words and then said, "SSS, eee, oh that word is See, right Grace?"

Grace nodded and Henry continued. "I know that word is Spot 'cause you read it in the other sentence. Grace smiled. Henry said, "The last word is run, just like on the top."

"That's it, Henry. Now put all the words together."

Henry read, "See Spot run."

Grace looked right at Henry and said, "Henry, you just read your very first sentence!"

"I did?"

"You did, and now, let's try the next page."

For over two hours, the children studied one page after another. Shortly after noon, Henry said, "Grace, don't read the last page. Let me read all of it, please."

"Sure," Grace replied. She was very pleased that Henry was picking up the words so quickly. He struggled over each new word but once he memorized the word, it was his to use in subsequent sentences. Grace had to admit that her little brother had a great memory and that would really help him in the learning to read process.

When Henry closed the back cover of the second book, he whispered to Grace, "I'm really getting hungry, Grace. Did you pack anything for us to eat?"

Grace leaned down and whispered, "We didn't really have anything, Henry. I think it's warming up a bit so let's take a walk and see if we can rustle up something to satisfy our growling stomachs.

While Henry busied himself putting on his coat and getting his backpack out from beneath the table, Grace put back the three Dick and Jane books in shelving unit A. Then, she zipped up Henry's coat and put on her own coat. After retrieving her backpack, the children headed out the library. When they came to the main part of the library, Miss Jefferson stopped them and said, "I swear I've never see children study so hard in all my life! Are you sure you don't want to just check out some books dear?" she asked, directing the question to Grace.

"Oh no mam, thank you but we won't be here for very long and I'd just as soon be in the library anyway. That is, if you don't mind." Our Nana is a pretty social lady and there's always someone at the house and it gets kinda noisy," she added.

Finally, Miss Jefferson gave a big smile and replied, "We don't mind a bit, Grace. You come in as often as you want and stay for as long as you want. We're a bit slow here during the holidays and you two are so well behaved!"

Those were exactly the words Grace was hoping to hear, especially the part a about staying as long as they wanted. "Thank you Miss Jefferson. We need to go get some lunch at Nana's house and then, we'll probably be back."

"You are most welcome, Grace. And sweetheart, it's Mrs. Jefferson."

"Sorry, well, thank you, Mrs. Jefferson. We'll see you later then."

The children exited the library. The sun was now midway in the sky and the air seemed decidedly warmer than when they had first arrived at the library. Henry turned to Grace and whispered, "Grace, I think we pulled it off."

Grace reminded Henry that he didn't have to whisper outside the library and she assured him that he had played his role just fine. Grace told her brother she was proud of his reading and that the more he read, the better he would get at reading even more difficult words.

When Henry asked where they would go for food, Grace told him that her friend Rosie said the large grocery at the corner of Main and Capitol oftentimes gave away samples of food. She said they would shop for a couple of grocery items and hope to "get lucky with the samples."

They rounded the corner of 7th Street West and Main and walked to the Super M Food Market. Grace was deciding what to buy that would not spoil and would also fit into her backpack. Henry poked her arm and pointed to a lady handing out samples of "little wieners." Grace approached the woman. The lady asked Grace if she and Henry would like to try one of her samples. She put a toothpick into two small wieners and handed them to the children.

Henry nearly swallowed his sample whole. He looked at the lady and said, "These are kinda small, mam. I couldn't really tell if I like them or not." Grace turned away so as not to laugh while the lady picked up another one and handed Henry another wiener. She asked Grace if she also would like another sample and Grace said she would like that. This time, Henry chewed the sample slowly and he said, "Ummm…that's really good, mam."

The lady said, "Be sure to tell your mother about them then. Tell her I have more samples if she'd like to try them before she buys." Henry told the sample lady that he would take a sample to his mother and the lady handed him two more "little wieners." The children assured the sample lady they would tell their mother about the delicious little wieners. As they walked off the lady called out, "Tell her they are specially made for the holiday parties."

Henry handed Grace one of the wieners and she ate it. Then, she pointed down another aisle, close to the dairy section. Another lady was handing out cheese and cracker samples. "Perfect!" Grace said to Henry as the two headed to the end of the aisle.

Each child was handed a cheese and cracker sample. Both children ate their samples slowly and then Grace said, "This is really good, mam. It might be what my mother needs for her Christmas Eve party. Is that a different kind of cheese there?"

"Oh we have several varieties young lady. Why don't you tell me which one you'd like to sample? Better yet, just take the ones you want to try."

Grace tentatively reached for one of the samples, distracting the lady while Henry skillfully swiped another sample of the cheddar spread crackers. "Now, just what one is this?" Grace asked.

Henry helped himself to another cheddar and cracker sample.

"Oh, that one is the pimento, dear. Some children don't

like it as well."

"Oh, I see the little pieces of olive in there. But, you know, I think adults might like this one really well. I'd better go tell my mother about these."

"Oh, here, dear, you really should sample the Swiss mixture.   It's new this year and a lot of people are raving about it!" While the lady pointed to the Swiss sample, Henry helped himself to two more samples of cheddar crackers. As Grace took the sample from the lady, the lady turned to Henry who had one sample stuffed in his mouth and another hidden in his left hand.

"Oh, dear, I didn't mean to ignore you, young man. Would you like to try another sample too?" Henry nodded his head and the woman handed him another cheddar cracker. Henry swallowed the sample in his mouth and said a weak, "Thank you, mam."

The children giggled as they walked away. Henry told Grace he could use something to drink. Grace looked around and then asked a stock clerk if there was a water fountain around. "Right up there by the restrooms, Miss," he said.

Henry ran to the fountain and gulped down water for a good thirty seconds. Then he stuffed the remaining two cheddar crackers in his mouth. "Man, those were good!" he declared to an amused Grace. Grace took a few drinks from the fountain and then told Henry they might want to buy a box of crackers and a jar of cheese spread to take with them. Henry thought that was a smashing idea! "Let's get cheddar if they have it, Grace," he urged.

As they walked around the store, they looked at various grocery items that they might want to buy for their library basement headquarters. They settled on the cheese and crackers along with two apples and two oranges. Grace reminded Henry that they still had "treats" in their backpacks. They went down the last aisle which was the bakery aisle. Henry ogled the pastries. Grace thought the aromas around the bakery aisle were heavenly. The smells reminded her of an imaginary grandmother's kitchen.

"Say there young man, could I interest you in a Christmas cookie?" a lady asked. The lady was behind the glass display case, wearing a white apron and a white hat on her head. Henry was a bit startled. When he composed himself, he looked at the lady and replied, "I don't have any money, mam."

"Well, isn't that just something then? You don't have any money and as it turns out, these here cookies are free. But just one to a customer," she said as she handed over a Santa cookie to Henry. Henry bit into the cookie just as Grace came up to the display and she immediately said, "Henry, you know we aren't supposed to eat treats in between meals!" Grace was afraid Henry had asked for the cookie and she did not want to waste the little money they had on treats.

The clerk immediately saw the problem and said, "Oh dear, I got a bit carried away. I'm sorry, child. We're handing out free Christmas cookies for the children while the parents shop. Here, why don't I put that young man's cookie in a bag and he can have it later. I'll put one in for you too, dear."

Grace was speechless! In about half an hour's time, she and Henry had nearly had a complete lunch and now, they were being offered dessert! She graciously thanked the pastry lady for the cookies as she took the sack the clerk handed over the counter. "Merry Christmas, children!" the pleasant lady called out as the two headed for the checkout counter. Both of the children waved and gave the store attendant generous smiles of appreciation.

Grace put the two apples, the two oranges, the jar of cheese and the small box of crackers on the counter. It came to just under a dollar. Their cash supply was dwindling.

Henry hung onto the sack of Santa cookies for dear life. When they exited the store, Grace took the items out of the grocery sack and put them into her backpack. When taken out of the bag, they seemed to fit better into the corners of her pack. She then folded up the grocery sack and put that in her pack as well. "Never know when it might come in handy," she said as Henry looked at her with a bit of curiosity in his face.

Grace said, "I gotta tell you, son, when it came to filling your belly, you didn't seem to be any too shy!"

At first Henry frowned and then he said, "Grace am I still playing my role in the play?"

Grace smiled and replied, "No, Henry, and I'm really glad you were a bit more assertive when it came time to filling your own needs. You are playing your role just perfectly!"

What's asserted mean, Grace?"

"Oh, assertion, well, it means that you go after what you want. And that was a great time to do it, Henry."

"So I didn't do anything wrong then?"

"You did nothing wrong, Henry and you did a lot of right things too. Acting inside the library is different than acting outside in the community, Okay? Now, what shall we do?" Do you want to look around the stores or something?"

Henry thought for a moment and then he said, "I think I want to go back to the library. I want to read more, Grace."

Grace was really pleased that Henry did not view the learning to read process as something boring. The library was warm and no one seemed the least bit suspicious of their prolonged presence there. They headed back up the street and up the steps of the Little Rock Carnegie Library.

"It's so good to be home again," Henry said matter-of-factly but with a mischievous grin on his face. Grace gave him a gentle poke on his arm and then put her right index finger to her lips. Henry immediately slipped back into the role of the shy little brother, lowering his head and holding onto Grace's hand.

Chapter Eight

When they entered the children's section, Mrs. Jefferson was nowhere to be seen. They removed their coats and placed their backpacks under the table as before. Then, they went to bookshelf A and Henry picked out two more Dick and Jane books to read. Grace asked if he wanted to try the Alice and Jerry Readers but Henry said he wanted to stick with Dick and Jane for a while longer.

They had been working together for about half an hour when a voice from in back of them asked, "Have a good lunch, kids?"

They turned to see Mrs. Jefferson behind them. "I had my lunch too. I see you're back at it," she said.

"Yeah, Nana had a meeting this afternoon so we told her we'd rather spend our time in here, if it's okay with you," Grace replied while Henry kept his head in the book.

"Like I said before, Grace, it's your library too!"

That statement produced a really wide grin on Grace's face. It was just what she had been hoping to hear. If the library was really part hers, she wasn't really trespassing. At least, that's the way she had figured it out to her own satisfaction.

At about mid-afternoon, Henry suddenly said, "Grace, I gotta pee – real bad, Grace."

Grace mentally kicked herself for not thinking of it earlier. "Okay, hang on, Henry. It's just back that way a bit." She hurried her brother toward the restroom. The last thing she wanted now was to have to clean up after an *accident*.

Fortunately, Henry made it in time. Grace went into the Ladies room while Henry went to the left to the door that said Men. When Grace came out, she momentarily panicked when she did not see Henry. Then, she looked down the room to the children's area and saw Henry already sitting quietly reading Dick and Jane. She watched as he hissed and aahed and tried to sound out each new word. She was so proud of Henry's motivation! Not only did Henry's effort promise to help him read, it also had the effect of disallowing anxiety in his small body.

Shortly before five o'clock, Mrs. Jefferson went to the children and tapped Grace on her right shoulder. Grace jumped and Mrs. Jefferson said, "I'm so sorry dear. I didn't mean to startle you but we'll be closing up the library soon."

"Oh my goodness! Time surely does fly when you're having fun, right Henry?" Grace replied. "We'll put away out books and head on out then. Thank you for your help, Mrs. Jefferson."

The librarian went around picking up books from other tables and returning them to their proper book stacks. Grace took Henry's books back to shelving unit A and then put on her own jacket. The children pulled out their backpacks and Grace helped Henry adjust his pack on his back. Grace made sure that Mrs. Jefferson saw them about to leave and she said, "Thanks again. Maybe we'll see you on Monday, Mrs. Jefferson."

"Hope so, children," Mrs. Jefferson said as she waved good-bye to them. Grace scanned the library and saw that Mrs. Jefferson was busy in the book shelving units. She quickly glanced to the front desk and noted that the librarian there was also engaged tidying up.

"Here's our chance, Henry," Grace whispered. She opened the door with the sign that said EXIT to ARCHIVES and the children hurried down the steps into a room which was literally covered with old book stacks.

"It smells weird, Grace," Henry commented as he looked right and left and then right again.

"That's the smell of old books, Henry. Let's go over there." Grace pointed to the left and started to lead Henry past dozens of bookshelves bulging with old books. Grace went to the far wall. "This is the front of the building, Henry. We can see if anyone is coming in through those two windows there." She pointed up to two small windows which appeared to Henry to be sealed shut.

"But won't they be able to look in and see us, Grace?" Henry asked.

"Henry, we're not going to sleep right here by the wall. We're going to be in about the middle of the book stacks. Let's wait a few minutes until the librarians leave and then we'll look for those cots I saw last time I was here."

The children sat on the concrete floor, with their backs against the wall. In about five minutes, they heard some talking and then, a door slammed. "One gone, one more to go," Grace said.

"I'm bored," Henry pouted.

"Henry..."

"Okay, Grace, but when will she leave?" Just then, they heard the sound of the front door being opened and then slammed shut. Grace thought she could hear the sound of the key being turned in the lock. She stood and jumped up so that she could get a glimpse out the window.

"She's gone, Henry. The place is ours now. At least until Monday," Grace added.

"Let's take off our backpacks and look around," Henry suggested.

"Good plan, little brother. Let me show you where the bathroom is down here."

"Can't we just use the one upstairs, Grace?"

"No, Henry. I don't want to go up there until it is unlocked on Monday. We could be arrested for trespassing." Grace totally ignored the fact that they were already trespassing but Henry seemed to accept her explanation.

Grace led Henry past the book stacks and into the right side of the basement. There were more book stacks there but not so many as on the left side. Some of the shelves held boxes. "Here's where the janitor keeps his cleaning supplies, Henry." Grace pointed to a small room to the right of where they were standing.

Curious to see the room, Henry headed in the open doorway and Grace heard him say, "Oh man, this is really something!"

Grace followed Henry into the room and saw him turning the crank on a very large bucket. "He must use that mop and bucket to clean up the floors, Henry."

Henry grabbed the rag mop and put it in the empty bucket, swishing it around as if it was filled with water. Then, he put the mop on the ringer mechanism and began to turn the crank as if he was trying to wring out the mop. "Maybe I could be a janitor when I grow up, Grace," he said with a smile of satisfaction on his face.

Grace thought to herself that it was just another one of those small things that so delighted her brother. "Come on, Henry, let me show you where the toilet is."

Grace pointed to another opening and they both went into a small room which contained a huge metal sink and a toilet.

"There's no bathtub, Grace," Henry observed with an expression of concern.

"Well, when we're away, we just need to take sponge baths then." When Henry continued to look concerned, Grace said, "That's when you just wash all over with a clean cloth and soap." It was at that exact moment that Grace remembered she had not thought to bring a bar of soap.

"I bet I could fit in that gigantic sink, Grace. I could take a bath in there."

"That might be a bit dangerous, Henry. I think we'll stay with the sponge baths for now," Grace replied.

"Is there a light in here, Grace?" Henry asked.

Grace went to the wall switch and pushed up the switch. The florescent lights came on and Grace immediately turned them off. They work just fine, Henry, but we'll use the flashlight at night because turning on the light might alert someone that we're down here.

"And we don't want that, do we, Grace?"

"Right Henry, we don't want that at all."

"Grace?"

"Yes, Henry?"

"You were right. This is a grand adventure. Henry went out of the supply room and began to run around the book stacks while Grace scouted out the supplies in the janitor's small closet. She found small drinking cups, paper towels and fortunately, a large bottle of hand soap which was obviously used to refill the hand soap dispensers in the upstairs bathroom. She looked around for clean sponges and found none.

Grace did come across a package of small, unused cleaning rags. "This will have to do for the sponge baths," she said to no one in particular. Satisfied that they had ample supplies to survive, Grace went back out to the book stacks to find Henry.

"Henry, where are you?" Grace called out.

"Gotta find me, Grace," Henry called back. Grace went in the general direction of where Henry's words had echoed. Just as she was about to spot him, he scooted around the end of the book stack and ran two stacks down. This continued for half an hour until all the book stacks had been navigated and there was nowhere else for Henry to go.

"This is a great place for playing hide and seek, isn't it, Grace?" Henry said, nearly out of breath from running from his sister.

"It's a goldmine, that's for sure, son," Grace said with an intentional aire of maturity.

"Hey, Grace?"

"Yes, Henry?"

"I like this side better. I like to be by this old cartoon boiler. It's nice and warm. It feels like all the arms are wrapping around me and keeping me safe. Can we sleep on this side instead?"

Grace's first inclination was to say no, but then she rethought her position and she said, "I don't see why not, Henry. It you feel better by the boiler, then this side it is! After all, we're partners in this adventure, right?"

"Yeah!" Henry screeched. Grace shushed him and then realized there was no one to hear them and she let it go.

"Did you see any cots when you were hiding from me Henry?" Grace asked.

"Oh, yeah, there're over there in the corner where the boiler is, Grace. Can we each pick out one?"

"Sure, but I'm sure they're all the same, Henry."

Henry ran to the stacks of folded cots and began to set up one after the other. When he had five cots lined up, he hopped on each one. "This one is the best, Grace. It's mine," he declared with a decided aire of authority.

Grace laughed and said, "Okay, Henry, put back three and leave one out for me."

"Don'tcha wanna try it out, Grace?"

"It'll be fine, Henry. You can get your blanket out of your backpack. I don't think we have anything for pillows though," Grace added.

"That's okay, Grace. We adventure people can just make do with what we have. I can use my jacket as a pillow."

Grace was amazed that Henry was becoming so resourceful. At home, he seemed timid and somewhat whiney. He had never liked to try new things. "That's a great idea, Henry! I think I'll use mine too. Or, I could use my sweatshirt, I guess."

The children began to set up their beds to their liking. When Henry was finished, he grinned at Grace and asked, "What's for dinner, chef?"

Grace smoothed out the blanket on her bed and answered, "Well, we have cheese and crackers and also an apple. I'd like to save the oranges for breakfast if that's okay with you, partner."

"My kind of dinner, partner!" Henry said, obviously very excited. "And can we have our Santa cookies for dessert, Grace?"

"Of course, partner. We wouldn't want them to go bad on us, would we?" Grace thought for a moment and then said, "Rats!"

"What's the matter, Grace?"

"I didn't bring a knife to cut the apple, Henry."

Henry was actually a wee bit happy that his older sister had not prepared for everything. He was going to say something disrespectful and then, he thought better of it.

"How about if we just take turns having bites then, Grace. I don't mind your cooties if you don't mind mine."

"I've never minded your cooties, Henry."

"How about drinks, Grace?"

"It will have to be water for us, Henry. We can get it out of the sink in there. I did find some small cups we can use. We have to remember to clean up anything we might use though."

After finishing up with their entrees of cheese, crackers and apple, the children bit into their cookies. "These are so good when they're fresh, aren't they, Henry?" Grace asked. Henry was too busy savoring the flavors of the sugar cookie coated with flavored icing to respond. Nevertheless he did nod vigorously.

After devouring his cookie, Grace suggested that Henry clean up and brush his teeth. Henry said it was too early to go to bed and Grace then offered Henry a choice. Either I can read you a story or we can play cards.

"Let's save the cards for tomorrow," Henry replied. "Do we have to stay in here all day, Grace?"

"Yes, we do, Henry. The doors are locked so that no one can get in to bother us. But, it also means we need to entertain ourselves down here until Monday morning at around eight o'clock in the morning. Tell you what. While you get ready for bed, I'll pick out a book from the stacks here. I'll read it to you until you fall asleep."

"Deal!" Henry said enthusiastically. He rummaged through his backpack and pulled out his pajamas, also pulling out a shirt and underwear in the process. "Oops," he said as he stuffed the excess items back into the bag.

While Henry got ready for bed, Grace began to browse through the book stacks. It was getting dark and she had to use the flashlight. She came to a stack of first edition children's book and knew she had hit the jackpot!

Grace pulled out a copy of The Swiss Family Robinson. She thought it might be just the adventure for Henry. It might also buoy up her spirits a bit as well. So far, her plan was going well, almost too well. Things that went too smoothly almost made Grace Gillian apprehensive.

When Henry came out of the janitor's storage room, Grace asked to see Henry's shirt and pants. She examined them carefully and then said, "Just wear these again tomorrow, Henry. They're pretty clean and we want to save our other clothes for when we need to go out.

"Should I wear the same underwear too, Grace?" Henry asked.

"Ummm…I think you should put on fresh underwear in the morning. Give me the ones you wore today and I'll rinse them out in the sink. I think they'll dry all right overnight and then you'll have a clean pair.

Henry tossed his used underwear in Grace's face and giggled.

"Not funny, son!" Grace remarked.

"Sorry, Grace. It probably has cooties on it too," he laughed.

Grace ignored the immature comments and she told Henry she had found a wonderful adventure book to read to him.

"What's it about? Is it scary, Grace?"

"It's about a family that is in a boat and the boat sinks and they end up on an island."

"Does anybody get killed or hurt real bad in the story?" Henry asked.

"No, Henry, they all survive and it's interesting to see what they do to entertain themselves. They are called the Robinsons and they are a bit like us. Of course, we're in a basement, not an island.

Henry thought for a moment and then said, "But still, we're kinda stranded, just like the Robinsons, huh, Grace?"

"Right. Now, I'm going to pull over my cot so I can be right near you. I am going to light a candle to save the flashlight batteries and then, I'll turn off the flashlight and read by candlelight."

"Just like Abe Lincoln, right, Grace?"

"Right, Henry, just like Abe Lincoln in his log cabin." Grace went to the janitor's room and got a metal bucket. She overturned it and set it at the head of her cot. Then, she put the candle on the top and lit it. It provided just enough light so that she could see the print but it did not glow so brightly so as to be seen on the other side of the book stacks. Grace was sure the light would not be seen from the window on the other side of the room. She was instantly grateful that Henry had suggested they camp at the back of the room rather than towards the front as she had initially planned.

First, Grace explained who the family members were and she then began to read Chapter 1. She told Henry that the Robinson's were on a ship when a storm came up and the ship hit some rocks. Since it was night, the family decided to stay on the ship as they could not see where they were.

In the morning, the four children explored the ship and they gathered things they might be able to use. The ship was still drifting a bit and the family hoped to find land soon.

Henry was completely taken by the story and he asked Grace if she thought they would get to land. Grace assured him that they would. She started Chapter 2 and sure enough, the family sited land. Not knowing what to expect, the parents suggested that they could take things from the ship to make themselves more comfortable until help arrived. Henry was visibly relieved to learn the family was safely on land. When Grace told about how the family made a tent from the sailcloth and they made beds from the island grasses, Henry was nodding his head as if the family was doing exactly what he would have done in their situation!

Grace could see Henry's eyes getting heavy but he was invested in the story and so she continued. She told Henry how the family explored the island looking for people, food and anything they could use to stay comfortable. "Just like us, huh, Grace?" Henry commented.

"Yup, just like us, son! But there are only two of us and there were six of them," Grace observed.

"Yeah, and two of them were grown-ups," Henry commented.

"Right again. But remember, Henry, the children are doing a lot on their own." When Grace got to the point that the children saw a dog kill a monkey, she hesitated whether or not to read it to Henry. She decided it was part of the story and she read it. Henry got teary-eyes but he said, "Grace, I'm so glad those children were there to take the baby and keep it safe."

Grace breathed a sigh of relief and she continued. Henry's eyes were now fluttering closed. When she began to read about the father and the son Fritz going back to the boat to gather animals that survived, Henry seemed content that the family was going to survive. He closed his eyes. When Grace heard a soft, steady rhythm to Henry's breathing, she closed the book, noting that she had left off at Chapter 5.

Getting out her own nightgown which was really an elongated tee shirt, Grace went to the janitor's room to clean up and brush her teeth. It was quite chilly in the storage room so she hurried with her tasks. She washed Henry's underwear and hung it over one of the boiler ducts. She walked to the front of the basement library and noted that the candle's glow was not visible there. She went back to the cots, blew out the candle and snuggled into her blanket. "Please let it work," she prayed as she closed her eyes and fell into a deep sleep.

Chapter

Nine

The library basement was relatively dark in the morning so

the children slept in. When Grace awoke, she could see

daylight streaming in from the front window and weaving in

and out of the book stacks. She had no idea what time it

might be. She felt rested and she was toasty warm.

Grace gazed up at the enormous boiler system and she

had to admit it looked a bit like a multitude of arms, all

protecting whatever was below. She chose to think of the

boiler as a friendly family of arms, all keeping her out of

harm's way. It had been a long time since she had felt that

sense of warmth and safety.

Grace remained on the cot and lavished in the freedom

from normal chores and demands. It was Sunday and no one

should be in the building. She was more grateful that others were locked out of the library than fearful that she and Henry were locked in. For the first time in a long time, Grace felt as if she and Henry had everything they needed right there in the basement of the Little Rock Carnegie Library basement. She hoped that the work week ahead would not put them in jeopardy of being found out. The library was her Plan A and she had no Plan B.

After a few minutes of basking in the short time between a feeling of twilight sleep and full alertness, Henry turned his head and, with a sleeping tone, asked, "Grace, do you think Mom will find us?"

Grace had been waiting for that question for the past day or so. She answered, "I expect we'll have to go find her, Henry. I don't think she'd think to look for us here."

"Do you think we should try to find her, Grace?"

"If it's important to you, we can walk back to the trailer park after tomorrow and see what's up. I don't want you to be too disappointed, son, but there's a good chance we won't see her for awhile."

"Do you think she just left us, Grace?"

"Well, I don't think she means to just leave us, Henry. Sometimes, her head just doesn't do what her heart says is right."

"Does she love us, Grace?"

"She does, Henry. She will always love us. But, sometimes, grown-ups just have trouble taking care of those they love, even if they want to. Do you know what I mean, Henry?"

"I think so. Some people are good at baseball or mathematics and some people are good at taking care of other people. Mom isn't so hot at that."

"Yeah, it's sorta like that, Henry. You gotta be able to take care of yourself before you can take care of someone else. And, I guess Lou Ann is still learning how to take care of herself."

"You're not like that, Grace. You already have taking-care-of-others skills. You're real good at it, Grace."

"Thanks, Henry. I think I learned it pretty young. Maybe about as soon as you came along."

"Was I easy to take care of, Grace?"

"Yeah, I'd say you were about average." Grace thought a moment and then added, "I guess you were above average, Henry, especially the last couple of days. In fact, I'd have to rate you way far ahead of most five year olds!"

"But Grace, I'm almost..."

"Oh for sure, you're almost six, Henry. I keep forgetting. It's only a month away now, isn't it?"

"Do you think Mom will be back for my birthday, Grace?"

"How about if we plan on just us two, Henry? And then, if Mom joins us, it'll be just an extra surprise!" Grace wanted to distract Henry from dwelling on the absence of his mother. She asked, "Shall we try some of our crackers for breakfast? Then, you get to choose what to do."

Henry got out of his bed and went into the bathroom. When he came out, he was dressed. He asked Grace if he could just look through the book stacks and Grace said that was a great idea. She said she wanted to browse as well.

After half an hour, Henry brought about half a dozen books for Grace to see. They were all children's picture books. "I want to look at these, Grace. Maybe I will know some of the words in them."

"Well, if you don't, I'll help you, son."

"What kind of books did you get, Grace?"

"These are all books on segregation, Henry. We're going to study it the next term in school. Maybe I can read ahead some and then it won't be so hard to understand when we study it."

"What's seg....gration?"

"It's called se...gre...gation, Henry."

"Yeah, so what's that, Grace?"

"I remember it, or at least a lot of it, Henry. Before we moved to the trailer park, I used to go to school where only white kids went. There were no children of color at my school."

Henry got a very confused look on his face and he asked, "Why?"

"They weren't allowed, Henry. They had their own school and they kept the colors separate. We couldn't go to the same schools or the same churches or the same restaurants or anything."

"Why?"

"I don't know for sure, Henry. But I heard some grown-ups talking about how colored people weren't as smart or as clean or as clever or something. I don't know how they figured that out but I know they're wrong."

"I know too, Grace. We only got me and two other white kids in my class and we all seem to think about the same. Now, I might be the first kid to read in my class but that's because you taught me, not because I'm white or brown or black or yellow."

Grace smiled. She was pleased that her little brother would not know some of the ugliness that beset people from one generation to the next.

"Can people who are colored think they're better than us, Grace?"

"Sure. Sometimes, I get called white trash by some of the uppity girls in my class, Henry. It hurts my feelings and I expect the people of color get their feelings hurt when someone tries to put them down as well."

"So, how did the schools get together then, Grace? I mean, how did they decide that people of all colors could go to the same school?"

"Let's look in this book, Henry. There are some pictures. See here, this is how it started according to the book. I'll tell you about it and then, if you have questions, you just ask, okay?"

"Okay, Grace."

"Well, back in 1954, there was a lawsuit. That's where people disagree and they take their arguments to a court and the judge decides what the right thing to do is."

Henry smiled and nodded that he understood the concept.

"Some Black children in the state of Kansas wanted to go to the public school because it was close to where they lived. Before, they had to take buses or walk a long distance to get to school and their parents didn't think it was safe or right that they couldn't just go to the school two blocks away. So the parents went to court. I guess their name was Brown. See, here's a picture of little Ruby Brown, Henry. She was only about your age. So, anyway, the judge decided the children had the right to go to the school closest to them and that started big problems with all the parents. Some of the schools up in the north didn't have a problem with the judge's decision but some of the schools in the southern states put up a real battle to keep the white schools white and the black schools black."

"Why? What difference does it make if your skin is brown or white? Don't we all need to learn the same things, Grace?"

"That's basically what the judge said, Henry, or rather, the Supreme Court judges in Washington, D.C. They said we should all have the same kind of knowledge."

"I hope our schools weren't the ones who said kids can't all learn together, Grace."

"Well, Henry, I hate to tell you this, but our schools here in Little Rock were sort of at the center of attention for awhile I don't know why but everyone just wanted things the same old way and they didn't want to change what was working."

"So what did they do?"

"They had to call in the National Guard to help, Henry."

"What's that, that guard thing?"

"Those are government troops that come into action if there's any kind of serious trouble in a state. They can help if there's flooding or tornadoes or riots. They were afraid that there might be terrible riots here and people would be hurt so they called in the government troops."

"And did the special school end then, Grace?"

"It took awhile but yes, Henry, the special schools ended and all different colored children could go to school together."

"Were the parents of the white kids mad that they lost, Grace?"

"Some were, most weren't. Some parents sent their kids to private school because they didn't want them going to schools that were not all-white."

"That's dumb," Henry said simply.

"I think so too, Henry, but back then, you have to remember that people were used to doing things in a certain way. Some people just aren't too much into changing what they think is working just fine."

"If different colors of kids went to different schools, it wasn't working just fine, Grace. Least ways, that's what I think"

"Maybe you should be a lawyer, Henry," Grace said with a tender smile of appreciation for her little brother's sensitivities.

"What's that?"

"Well, a lawyer is someone who goes into the courtroom and argues for what he or she thinks should be done. Sometimes, if they argue really well, the laws get changed. That's what happened with the schools, Henry."

"I don't think I can argue that good yet, Grace."

"Well, give yourself time, Henry. First, you got to learn to read and then…"

"Then, I can be a lawyer and I'll know just the right things to say to win my case, right, Grace!"

"Right, Henry," Grace said as she laid the book aside. At eleven years of age, Grace understood that you just shouldn't flood young children with things they didn't even ask to know.

"Grace?"

"Yes?"

"Did they the get animals from the ship?"

"Oh," Grace said in recognition of Henry's reference to last night's story. "Sure they did, son. They got a pig and I think they got a donkey and some sheep too."

"How do you get animals from the ship to the beach, Grace?"

"I know they did something, Henry. Shall we read some more of the story now?"

"Let's wait until tonight, Grace. Can we play some cards now?" Henry asked.

"Sure we can. What do you like?

"How about war, Grace? Let's make the Jacks and Kings the army, okay?"

"Why all men?"

"Okay then, Jacks and Queens," Henry replied.

The children spent well over an hour slapping Jacks and Queens and taking the card piles to their own piles of cards. Finally, Henry said, "Let's see if I can read one of those books, Grace."

Henry looked through his pile of books and got one that had large lettering in the text. Grace thought it was an interesting choice but she said nothing. It was a Christmas book and she knew Henry must be wondering if Santa would find them this year.

Grace put their blankets on the floor next to the octopus boiler and the two sat down to read. Henry opened the book and studied the first picture. "It says THE here, Grace."

Grace patted Henry on the back and asked if he needed help with the next words. Henry frowned and then nodded.

"It's a hard word, Henry. See, they try to trick you by putting the G next to the T and that makes it hard to sound out. Just forget about the G and try to sound it out without that letter," Grace suggested.

Henry struggled and then asked, "Is it Nity, Grace?"

Grace smiled but was careful not to laugh. "No son, the E is silent."

"They tried to trick me again, didn't they, Grace?" Henry asked. He had a charming smile and Grace just couldn't resist loving her little brother just a little bit more.

"They did, Henry. They tricked me that way when I started to read too," she said with a voice filled with compassion.

Then she added, "Say the letter I just that way, Henry. It's called a long I because you said it just like you pronounce the letter."

Henry initially frowned and then his face lit up! "It's NIGHT isn't it, Grace?!

Grace raised her right arm into the air with a salute of victory. "That's it, Henry! You are really a good student," she added.

"So then, it says THE NIGHT then, right?"

"Right, son. It's THE NIGHT BEFORE...what?" she asked, giving her brother a hint in reward for his persistence."

"Grace," Henry said with a look of disgust on his face. "You read the next word and I was 'spose to do it."

Grace had to grin. It was getting harder and harder to finesse Henry. "Sorry," she said meekly.

"Well, so it has to be THE NIGHT BEFORE CHRISTMAS, right?"

"Right." Grace said without further elaboration.

"So, I guess they musta tricked us again then?"

Grace gave Henry a look of curiosity and Henry then said, "They put a T in Christmas to try to trick us, but I guess the T is silent just like the E, right, Grace?"

Henry struggled to the end of the first page and then asked his sister to read the book to him. As she read, Henry followed the words with his eyes. He was in deep concentration when he asked, "Grace, what's a sash?"

"It's the bottom part of the window, son. Old houses used to have shutters on the inside for extra protection. To, to open the window, you needed to first put back the shutters and then you could reach down to the window sash to open the window."

Henry nodded his understanding as Grace continued. After the phrase "As dry leaves before the wild hurricane fly, when they meet with an obstacle, mount to the sky," Henry asked the meaning of the phrase

Grace put the book on her lap and looked into the curious eyes of her brother. "Henry, it makes me so happy that you ask questions when you don't know the answers. You are becoming a real scientist. That's how they figure out things. So, that means that the reindeer and St. Nicholas's sleigh were dashing up to the rooftops like leaves caught up in the wind. And, by the way, coursers in this poem mean reindeer."

"I figured that out last year when I heard it in preschool, Grace," Henry said matter-of-factly.

Grace picked up the book and was about to finish the poem when Henry asked, "So, you don't mind if I ask question, Grace? I mean I don't have to act in the role you gave me when just we two are together?

"That's right, Henry. When, it's just us, you can ask me anything you want."

"Okay then," Henry said as he took a deep breath.

Grace got a quizzical look on her face as Henry looked directly into her eyes and asked, "Are we orphans now, Grace?"

Grace literally gasped! She had no idea Henry was so perceptive. He was just a little boy. He shouldn't have such ugly and frightening thoughts in his head. She wasn't sure she knew what to say but she knew she had to at least try.

"Henry," she said with a look of compassion, "our mother wasn't always like this. She used to have a job and she took care of me, well, us. You were too little to remember."

"So, what happened then?" Henry asked with a bit of defiance in his voice."

"I don't know, son. I think life just began to wear her down. It does that to some people, Henry."

"Is that why she drinks that stuff and goes to sleep?"

"That's kinda the way I figured it out, Henry. Life got too much for her and she uses the bottle to take away the fears or the pain or something like that. It's sorta like a sickness, I guess."

"Why doesn't she go to the doctor if she's sick?"

Grace had to think about that one for awhile. It was a very good question. Finally, she looked Henry squarely in the eyes and said, "I guess maybe it's easier. It takes away the pain for awhile and then, you just go out and try again. Pretty soon you get so used to taking away the pain that way that it just becomes a part of your life."

"I hate it," Henry replied with his mouth clenched.

"I do too, Henry." There was little else Grace could say as her brother had summed up their feelings in a very simple and succinct way.

Grace was hoping that Henry's curiosity was quelled for the moment but he continued. "So, what if she doesn't come back, Grace? What's our next plan?"

That was a question Grace Gillian hoped would never be asked. Now that it had been asked, she struggled to formulate a response that might appease her brother for the moment.

"That's why we're here, Henry. We need thinking time and this is just the place to do some good thinking. It's warm and it has a lot to stimulate our brains. And even better, there's no one to bother us."

Henry studied his sister for a moment and then asked, "Grace, could you finish the book? Maybe it will give us some ideas."

Grace was never so happy to end a discussion as at that moment. "So up on the housetop…..." she continued.

When the story was ended, both of the children remained silent until Henry spontaneously reached over to hug his sister. Grace was surprised but she returned the hug.

"I got an idea, Grace," Henry said. "We gotta go back and see Santa," he said with a grin.

Chapter

Eleven

The children spent the rest of the weekend playing cards,

reading books and playing hide-and-seek in the book stacks.

When they went to bed on Sunday evening, Henry had

already extracted a promise from his sister that they would go

back to the department store the next day and allow Henry

another chance to chat with Santa.

Early Monday morning, Grace and Henry got up, ate

most of their food and put back the cots in their rightful

places. Grace scrutinized the area before she quietly led

Henry up the stairs. She had heard someone unlocking the

front door and she knew that the library was officially open at

nine AM. At exactly ten minutes after nine, Grace quietly

opened the EXIT door and looked around the front of the

library. She knew the librarian was there but she was not able to spot her location.

Then, Grace and Henry heard voices which appeared to be coming from the children's library area. "I think she's talking to Mrs. Jefferson, Grace," Henry concluded.

Grace whispered, "That's perfect, Henry. Let's go out now and go to that area. They'll think we just came in the front door."

The children approached the area where the two librarians were chatting. Talia Jefferson immediately spotted them and waved, saying, "Oh my, aren't you two up bright and early!"

Henry and Grace approached them with smiles and Henry went immediately to Book stack A while Grace approached the librarians.

"Betty, this is Grace and her little brother Henry is over there getting his books. Grace is staying with her grandmother over the holidays and she's teaching her little brother how to read."

Betty smiled and said to Grace, "How nice to meet you, child. I'm Betty Drummel. If there's anything I can do to help you out, just let me know."

Grace thanked her and was about to go help Henry when Betty asked, "Say, Grace, just who is your grandmother, dear? I think I know about everyone in this town now."

Grace shuttered and then regained her composure. She turned her head slightly as she said, "I doubt you've met her yet, Mrs. Drummel. She just moved here a couple of months ago. It was just after my grandpa died. I guess she has friends here or something," she added as she scurried off to meet up with Henry."

Betty shrugged and told Talia she needed to put back some books in the stack. She exited the children's area and Talia busied herself with her own duties.

The children again spent the morning with Dick and Jane. By noon, Henry was able to read most of the books with relative ease and Grace told him time and time again how proud she was. Henry beamed and then reminded his sister that it was "Time to run some errands."

The books were put back in the stacks and on the way out, Grace informed Mrs. Jefferson that they'd be back in the afternoon if their grandmother didn't need them for household chores.

"How's Henry doing, Grace?" Mrs. Jefferson asked.

"He's a natural, Mrs. Jefferson, Grace replied. Then, adding a note of authenticity, she added, "If we can get back this afternoon, he's ready to start on the Alice and Jerry Readers.

Mrs. Jefferson smiled as the children headed for the front door. She saw them head to the restroom and then she headed back to her own desk.

Once outside, Henry said, "She's really nice, isn't she, Grace?"

"Very nice," Grace replied. "Where to first?" she asked.

"Let's try that grocery store again, Grace. My tummy is growling and I need to satisfy it before we go to see Santa." He looked toward Grace, hoping she had remembered her promise of a second visit the previous evening.

Apparently she had as she replied, "Maybe you could even get another treat bag, Henry! They probably won't even remember us."

They headed to the main street and went directly to the supermarket. "I think we hit the jackpot, Grace!" Henry said as they saw close to a dozen venders handing out samples.

"Well, tomorrow night is Christmas Eve and people are probably buying up things for parties and dinners, Henry. I imagine the vendors want to encourage sales of their own items, don't you suppose?"

Henry nodded and headed for a small table where the aroma was drawing him in. "What are those?" he asked the sample lady.

"This is something new, young man. We call them chicken fingers and I happen to think they're the best thing ever invented in the food department. When nothing was offered, Henry looked at the lady and said, "Well, they can't be better than drumsticks, mam."

That was all the challenge the sample lady required as she handed a platter out to the children, saying, "Here take one and let me know what you think."

Henry gobbled his chicken finger in two bites as Grace took her time, frowning from time to time. "I can't quite figure out what this stuff is on the top," she said to the sample lady.

While Grace and the lady chatted about breading and spices, Henry helped himself to another two samples.

"You know, I think my mother just might want to try

this. She's having a Christmas Eve party tomorrow night and she's been looking for something new.

"Well, here then," the sample lady said. "Here's another one for you and take these for your mother. If she likes them, they're in the packages right over there," she said as she pointed to a refrigerated area just across from her sample table.

Grace thanked the lady and the children headed to the cheese table. A different lady was handing out samples so the children felt confident they wouldn't be recognized from their sampling session on Friday. Henry charmed the lady, asking about the various cheeses and how they might be cut into Christmas designs by use of cookie cutters and such.

When the children had their fill of cheese samples, Henry said, "Oh, look, Grace, Mom's over there! Let's tell her about the cheese!" And they scurried down an aisle and out.

They sampled fruit platters and vegetable platters and ended up at the hot chocolate table. "Are these samples?"

Henry asked politely.

"No son, we're just giving them out to the shoppers. There's a bit of a nip in the air today and we just figured people might appreciate sipping as they shopped. Want some?" she asked.

Henry gave the lady his biggest smile and said, "Yes please, I would." "Marshmallows?" she asked.

Henry nodded his head in appreciation of the additional treat and then said, "And my sister would like one too, please. She's kinda shy. Well, really not shy, I guess. She just doesn't like to ask for things."

The lady smiled and handed both children paper cups filled with hot chocolate and marshmallows. "There are waste baskets around the store. You can just toss the empty cups in any one of them" she added.

The children thanked her and went to the front of the store where management had placed several benches for weary shoppers. They couldn't believe their luck.

"Do we even need groceries, Grace?" Henry asked as he sipped his hot chocolate. He sighed in appreciation of its warmth.

"We'll just pick up a couple of things, Henry. We'll probably be hungry by tonight."

"Do we still have crackers and peanut butter?" Henry asked.

"Yeah, but not much, son. How about a couple pieces of fruit?"

"I'll think about that, Grace. Let's look around some more. Maybe we should look over by the bakery," Henry suggested.

Grace was thinking her little brother was becoming quite the schemer. When they finished their drinks and then tossed the empty cups in the trash cans, they headed toward the bakery section. They hadn't been there more than ten seconds when a cheery voice said, "Here, children, over here. We're passing out free Christmas cookies, you know."

Henry grinned from ear to ear. He and Grade went to the glass counter. This time, they were allowed to pick out their own cookies.

Henry studied the four varieties with intensity and finally said, "I'd like the Santa one, please."

The bakery lady picked up the cookie and placed it in a small bag and then asked, "How about you, young lady? You're never too old for a Christmas cookie!"

Grace blushed a little and then smiled and said, "That reindeer looks mighty pretty, mam." Her cookie was also placed in a small sack and the children both thanked the baker and left the area.

"We'll save these, right, Grace?"

Grace nodded her head and they wandered the store for a few minutes. Henry pointed to a sign and asked, "What's that mean, Grace? It says D-E-L-I. It that a trick word again?"

"It says DELI, Henry. But, I'm not sure what that is. Must be something new. Shall we take a look-see?"

Henry was game so he and Grace wandered over to the area. People were in a small line being waited upon. The children stared through the glass and finally, Henry said, "Look, Grace. They already made up the food for the people."

Grace studied the items and finally said, "I guess you just have to heat it up and you have your dinner, Henry."

"Well, only the hot things, Grace."

"Huh?"

"You only heat up the hot things, Grace. You don't heat up the potato salad and the cold slaw."

Grace ignored her brother as she continued to study the food items. Unknowingly, they had joined the line of customers.

"And what'll it be for you, little lady?" the clerk asked.

Grace was startled as she realized she was being addressed as a customer. She quickly glanced at all the items and then asked, "Would that chicken keep for a while, sir?"

"Oh, yes, miss. It's fully cooked already. Fact of the matter is, I just put mine in the frig and eat it cold. It's delicious that way."

"Well, how much would two drumsticks be then?" Grace asked.

"They're a quarter apiece, Miss, or three for fifty cents. We charge more when we have to do the preparation, you understand."

Grace looked at Henry and then she said, "We'll take two then, sir."

Henry looked amazed but he said nothing.

The drumsticks were wrapped and handed to Grace and she asked where she should pay for them. She was told she should pay at the check-out counter up front.

They went to the check-out counter and Grace paid for the chicken. When they were outside, Henry finally asked, "Isn't that a lot of money, Grace?"

Grace held the bag in one hand and she took Henry's hand in hers as she said, "It's almost Christmas, Henry. And besides, we both need something to keep up our strength."

"But we don't have a refrigerator, Grace," Henry protested.

"The storage room isn't heated Henry. It's nice and cool in there," Grace replied. And they headed off to see Santa.

Chapter Twelve

When they entered the department store, they were
immediately warmed. Henry wanted to use both the
elevators and the escalator so Grace humored him, saying it
was all part of the Christmas Spirit. Henry broke free from
Grace's hand and began to run toward the escalators.

"Henry!" Grace called out with decided authority in
her voice. Henry turned around and immediately felt guilty
for his own sense of freedom. He waited for Grace to catch up
to him and then said, "Sorry, Grace."

"I know you're excited, Henry, but we have to stay
together. It's all part of the plan, son," Grace said. She then
took Henry's hand and made sure he was safely on the bottom
step of the escalator and then said, "Let's see if you can get off
at the top on your own, okay?"

Henry was pleased that Grace recognized he was no longer a baby and it had not escaped Grace's attention that her little brother appeared to be maturing before her very eyes these past few days.

"How'd I do?" Henry asked proudly as he stepped off carefully at the top of the escalator run.

"Perfect!" Grace said with praise. "Want to go down or go to the elevators now?"

"I want to see Santa, Grace. There might be a long line today," Henry said with his most serious tone of voice.

Grace shrugged, took Henry's hand and headed toward the Winter Wonderland display where Santa had his greeting area.

As expected, there was a long line and Grace and Henry noticed unruly children not doing well with their own impatience. Grace gave Henry a stern look and he immediately understood that he was not to join in their antics.

"Why do you need to go again, Henry? Did you forget to tell Santa something?" Grace asked.

"Yeah, something like that." Not wanting to withhold information from his sister, Henry added, "It kinda has something to do with the plan, Grace."

"Is it some kind of back-up plan, Henry?"

"No, I know you'll be in charge of that Grace. It's sorta like a booster shot to whatever plan we have."

That got Grace curious but she decided not to pursue it what with all the people around to listen in. Instead, she said, "Looks as if they're giving away sacks again, Henry."

"Maybe I shouldn't take one, Grace. I got one already."

"If it's offered, it's okay, son," Grace said with a gentle smile. That second sack of goodies just might be the sum total of Henry Gillian's Christmas.

*****

It took nearly forty minutes to reach the front of the line and Henry and Grace were tired of standing and being bumped by the other children. When Henry went to the raised area to talk with Santa, Grace got out of line and went to the side of the stage area to wait for Henry. He seemed to be spending more than his share of time with Santa. At one point, Henry whispered something in Santa's ear. Grace looked attentively as Santa first smiled and then nodded to Henry.

An elf came to take Henry down the steps and Henry was handed a bag of goodies. Henry looked inside the sack and then whispered to the elf that looked in Grace's direction. The elf then handed Henry a second sack.

Henry strutted toward Grace like a toy soldier in a Christmas parade. He looked truly proud of whatever it was he has just accomplished. Grace did not want to be intrusion. She immediately suggested they take their journeys on the elevator and the escalators.

After three trips up and down the elevators and escalators, Grace suggested they might want to get on back to the library.

"Could I start the Alice and Jerry Readers, Grace?"

"I don't see why not, Henry. I think the temperature is dropping so we'd best be on our way."

"How do you know about the temperature, Grace?"

"Just look at the shoppers coming in, Henry. They have snow on their hats and they are all giving that 'burrrrrrr' shaking motion when they step inside the doors.

Henry looked at the new shoppers. Then, he buttoned up his coat and put on his stocking cap and they literally ran back to the library.

Chapter

Thirteen

The library was beginning to feel like a welcome home

to the two wandering children. Grace insisted Henry use the

bathroom when they entered the front doors. She used the

facilities as well. When she came out, she peeked toward the

back of the library and saw that Henry had already pulled

some books and was sitting at the table trying to decide which

book to read.

As Grace headed toward the children's section, she ran

into Mrs. Drummel and she mentally prepared herself for an

inquisition. Betty Drummel had immediately stuck Grace as

the type of woman who wanted to know everything about

everybody and she was potentially a trouble-maker if she got

too much information

"Well, hello there, Grace," Mrs. Drummel said. "Did you and Henry have a good lunch?"

Grace smiled and replied, "Oh, yes, Mrs. Drummel. My Nana is a wonderful cook. She asked if Henry and I would like to shop with her this afternoon but we told her we were making so much progress with Henry's reading that we wanted to return to the library."

"And just where does your grandmother live, dear?" Mrs. Drummel inquired.

Grace had already had enough and she decided to end the conversation quickly. "She lives just a couple of blocks away, Mrs. Drummel. Now, I need to get back to Henry, Mrs. Drummel. I promised Nana I wouldn't leave him alone you know," she said as she scurried back to where Henry was seated.

Mrs. Drummel shrugged and went back towards the front of the library to do whatever it was she did.

Grace saw Henry choose a new book in the Alice and Jerry Readers series. It was one of the pre-reader books and Grace felt confident that Henry would ace that book. There was a dog named Jip in the book and Henry easily sounded out the dog's name. In fact, he read the entire book out loud to Grace and only need a slight prompt on one word.

As soon as that book was finished, Grace picked out a book in the first grade series. Henry needed a bit of assistance but for the most part, he was actually reading by himself!

By midafternoon, Henry had told his sister that she needed to pick out books for herself as he no longer needed any help. Grace said, "Henry James, I am *SO* proud of you! You're going to be the best first grade reader in the class!"

Henry was so engrossed in the new story that he just glanced up at Grace and smiled. Grace had the feeling that despite their circumstances, something good was in the wind for her brother. He was such a charming little boy. Grace thought to herself that anyone would want Henry Gillian.

Chapter Fourteen

The library closed for the night and Grace and Henry again managed to get through the EXIT door and down to the basement without being seen.

Grace immediately took out the drumsticks from her backpack and put them into the cool storage area, hoping to keep them fresh for a Christmas Eve dinner for Henry and herself the following night.

They had peanut butter and cracker sandwiches for dinner and Grace then shared the remaining orange with Henry. As a special pre-Christmas treat, they both ate their candy canes while Henry looked through the bag he had gotten from Santa that afternoon.

"Look, Grace, they put a yo-yo in my bag!" Henry squealed in delight.

Grace took out the bag the elf had given her and she said, "I got one too. Do you know how to use it, Henry?"

Henry shook his head so Grace then gave her brother a demonstration on how to keep the yo-yo in motion. Within ten minutes, Henry was a pro and he obviously got a lot of pleasure from his athletic prowess.

Grace studied her brother and thought how much he had grown during their few days in the library. She almost had to laugh when she realized that Henry seemed to be better off without the uncertainty of his mother. But then, she chastised herself for placing Henry in another situation which was equally as uncertain. As soon as they were found out – and she knew it would be soon – well, then, Henry's anxiety was sure to return with a vengeance.

Grace calculated what was left of their money. She wanted very much to get something special for Henry for Christmas. Maybe they could go back to Macy's tomorrow and she could pick out something. He didn't seem to require much to keep him happy. They had to stop at the grocery store as well and maybe if they were lucky, there would be another Christmas cookie for her brother. It would be a meager Christmas for them but at least, there would be more love than money could buy.

That night, Grace tucked Henry in and read to him from the Swiss Family Robinson book. The Robinson's were now making tools and other things to sustain them on the island. They had built a hut for the animals and the tools and they begin to plant a garden. As he dosed off to sleep, Henry commented, "I think we're doing about as good as them, Grace."

Grace kissed her brother on the cheek and went to the storage room to clean up. She washed Henry's clothes and placed them over one of the arms of the octopus boiler. She lay down on her cot and ruminated for hours before going to sleep. In her dreams, the octopus boiler arms had turned into social service workers who were removing her and Henry from the stability of their basement hideaway.

As she awakened the following morning, Grace Gillian had feelings of foreboding that would remain with her throughout the day.

Chapter Fifteen

Grace was pensive upon awakening. Her dream had seemed all too real and she was genuinely afraid for her brother and herself. She had no alternative plan for safety and even if they managed to avoid detection during the holiday, they had nowhere to go when the school term began in January.

Grace put out the remaining food and told Henry to take whatever he wanted. She was saving the drumsticks for the evening so she hid them in a place where the janitor was not likely to discover them.

The children waited until twenty minutes after nine so as not to appear too quickly upstairs. Just as they came through the EXIT door, Mrs. Jefferson appeared looking startled.

"Oh my goodness, you two scared me to death!" she said.

"Oh, I'm so sorry, Mrs. Jefferson," Grace said pleasantly. "We just got here and Henry had to use the restroom," she explained.

"Oh, of course, dear. You go right ahead now. You do know we close early today, don't you?"

Grace initially looked concerned but then thought that might actually be a good thing for herself and Henry.

"I didn't know that, Mrs. Jefferson. What time will you close?"

"We close at three o'clock today, dear. Actually, the staff is having a little Christmas celebration then. We'd love to have you and Henry join us if you could. That is, if your grandmother can spare you two," she added with a grin.

Before Grace could get out a reply, Henry eagerly asked, "Oh, could we, Grace? Will you have cookies and things?" Henry asked as he jumped up and down with excitement.

"Henry!" Grace admonished. Then she had pangs of guilt. Henry was just a little boy and what did she have to offer to him on Christmas? She smiled and then said, "Tell you what, son, we'll go out, run our errands and then see if it's okay with Nana, okay?"

"But, Grace…," Henry said. He looked at his sister and immediately recovered and went back to *the plan*. "Oh, yeah, we need to check to see if Nana wants us to help with the Christmas Eve party or if she just wants us out of her hair, right?"

"Oh, don't make it a problem," Talia Jefferson said. "We'd love to have you here. We're all so proud of you two. It's not many big sisters that would take the time to help their little brother learn to read over a holiday. It's just that, well, we all think you're both pretty special.

Grace looked from Mrs. Jefferson to Henry and then back to Mrs. Jefferson. "Tell you what, Henry, let's run our errands a little early today and then we'll have time to check in with Nana around noon. If she gives us the okay, we'll be back just after lunch. Would that be okay, Mrs. Jefferson?"

Talia Jefferson nodded and then Grace said, "Well, one way or another, we'll let you know then. Henry, we'd better hit those book stacks. It's probably going to be the last day we get to use the library," she said somberly.

Henry gave Grace a look of concern as she gently eased him back toward the children's section.

When they were seated, Henry asked, "Grace do we have to move?"

"I don't know, Henry. There are a few days of vacation after Christmas but I don't know if we're going to be able to stay without being found out. Let me think about it, okay?" Grace asked.

Henry began to shake and Grace took him behind the book stacks and held him to her chest and stroked his head. "Look Henry, we're still having the adventure and we both need to play our roles. Let's just assume now that we'll be here for another few days, okay?"

That seemed to calm Henry and Grace relaxed just a bit. She urged Henry to get some more books and then told him that they would leave the library late morning to go to the grocery store and maybe, even go back to Macy's. That cheered up Henry and he became more animated as he began to browse the Alice and Jerry Readers selection.

Grace selected a Jane Austin novel and then instructed Henry to remind her when the little hand on the clock got to the number eleven.

Chapter Sixteen

Talia Jefferson made several phone calls during the morning. On occasion, she would glance at the children sitting at the table, intent on growing toward their own excellence.

As soon as the small hand of the clock was on the eleven, Henry reminded Grace they were to leave early. They put away their books. Grace mentally made a note of the page on which she left off reading.

On the way out of the library, the children greeted both Mrs. Jefferson and Mrs. Drummel. Both women seemed to be in an unusually good mood and they told the children they hoped they would see them for the library party later in the day.

"Where to first, son?" Grace asked as they made their way down the steps of the library.

"Could we go look at the trailer, Grace?" Henry asked.

Grace had feared Henry would ask that. She had been waiting for it. "Okay," she said with as much composure as her eleven-year-old mind would allow.

They made their way down 7th Street for several blocks and then turned right and walked two blocks on State Street. They stopped in front of the mobile home park entrance and looked toward the trailer in which they had lived just the past week. For Grace, it seemed ages ago, a different time and a different place. She and Henry had both changed a lot since the day they left the cold, unwelcoming trailer home.

"There's someone else moving in, Grace," Henry said with a frown.

"Yeah, it's not ours anymore, Henry."

"Do you think Mom has a place to live?"

"Yes, I do, Henry. Somewhere, she is safe and warm."

"Let's go to Macy's first," Henry said and he took Grace's hand as they made their way to the downtown area.

They did their customary elevator and escalator rides but the motion did not seem to have the thrill it had the day before. They walked through the Winter Wonderland but somehow, it no longer felt as if they belonged in such a magical place. Grace asked Henry if he would like to talk with Santa again but Henry declined. Grace had a feeling that their grand adventure was somehow closing in on them. Furthermore, she was getting tired of lying.

The children stopped by the supermarket and got some samples, more as a necessity than as a treat. Grace purchased a box of sugared cereal they could eat dry and then, she got two apples for Christmas dinner.

After their errands, the children walked slowly back to the library, returning around one-thirty. Henry immediately went to the book stacks and pulled three books to read. Grace excused herself, saying she needed to use the restroom. She sought out Mrs. Jefferson who was busy with paperwork at her desk.

"Well, hello, dear. Did you and Henry have a good outing?" Mrs. Jefferson asked.

"Yes, it was lovely, thank you. I wanted to ask you a question, Mrs. Jefferson," Grace replied.

"Certainly, dear."

"I was wondering if you ever sell any of the books you have here."

When Mrs. Jefferson frowned with confusion and failed to reply, Grace explained, "I want to buy my brother a book for Christmas. I didn't save enough for a new book and I noticed that you have several copies of some of the books. I was just wondering if maybe I could buy one for Henry."

Talia Jefferson smiled and then asked, "Which one were you interested in buying, Grace?"

"Well, I see you have three copies of a couple of the Wonder Story Books and I'm thinking Henry will soon be ready for them. You have four copies of "It Happened One Day. Maybe you could spare that one," Grace replied.

Mrs. Jefferson rose from her desk and went back to the book stacks. She returned holding a copy of the book Grace had named and said, "You're right, Grace, we seem to have one too many of this particular book. How about if we just donate it to Henry's reading cause?" she said.

Grace noticed that Mrs. Jefferson had picked out the best copy of the book. "Oh no," she replied. "It wouldn't be a gift for my brother if my work didn't help to pay for it. I earned the money cleaning for people before when…" Grace paused and then said, "Well before we came for vacation with Nana."

Talia Jefferson struggled to hold back tears. She maintained eye contact with the sturdy and compassionate young lady before her and said, "Okay then, I guess the library board would appreciate 25 cents for the book. It will be put into the fund to purchase more books, Grace."

"It's a deal!" Grace said with an appreciative smile.

"I have some wrapping paper in the office if you'd like to wrap it for Henry, dear.

"Grace produced a generous grin and replied, "That would be wonderful, Mrs. Jefferson." For the first time that day, the feelings of foreboding were placed in the deeper recesses of Grace Gillian's mind.

Grace followed Mrs. Jefferson to the staff office. She was shown the choices of wrapping paper and then given a bow for the outside of the package. When Grace finished wrapping the book, she thanked Mrs. Jefferson and went quietly back to the children's section and tucked the book into her backpack. Henry was still reading and hardly noticed when Grace sat across from him with her own book.

Chapter Seventeen

At precisely three o'clock, Talia Jefferson interrupted the children and told them it was time to begin the Christmas party. Grace and Henry placed their books back in the shelves and picked up their backpacks and coats. Mrs. Jefferson told them they should just put their personal possessions in the office so that everything would be together when they left the library for the day.

After placing their backpacks and coats in Mrs. Jefferson's office, the librarian led the two children to a large room where several people already sat in chairs. There was a small, decorated tree in the corner with gifts placed underneath. Grace figured that the gifts were fake and simply there for the effect.

Grace and Henry were introduced by Talia Jefferson as "special honored guests." Then, Mrs. Jefferson introduced six staff members and their families. There were two children there about the ages of Grace and Henry and that put the two guest children more at ease.

When they were introduced to the janitor and his wife and two children, Henry stared intently at the man. Grace was about to chide him for being rude when Henry's attention was drawn to a long table on which cupcakes, pudding, drinks and other Christmas treats were placed. His eyes were as wide as saucers and indeed, Grace herself had never seen such a display of Christmas wonder all seemingly there for the pleasure of the guests. And, she and Henry were two of the quests! She was immediately intensely happy for her brother. There would be a Christmas celebration after all!

Everyone was urged to help themselves to the Christmas goodies and Grace and Henry almost felt themselves to be a part of the group. Whenever anyone asked about their grandmother, both children spoke with ease about how "Nana is making the final preparations for her party tonight and she was *sooo* happy to get us out of her way!"

After everyone had filled up on holiday goodies, a tall man stood up to thank the staff for their wonderful work at the library that year. Mrs. Jefferson leaned over and whispered that he was Mr. Valentine, the president of the Library Board of Directors. He had greying hair and his stature was almost regal. He looked every bit the part of the president.

After Mr. Valentine finished his thank-yous to the staff, he began to get the presents from beneath the tree to hand out to everyone. The children immediately opened their gifts and thanked the library board profusely. If anyone forgot their manners, the parents were quick to whisper instructions and the children immediately complied.

When everyone had a gift, Grace noticed that not all of

the gifts from under the tree had been passed out. She

thought someone probably had not been able to show up for

the party. Or, maybe, they were decorations after all.

Mr. Valentine cleared his throat and then said that Mrs.

Jefferson had brought to his attention an act of library

citizenship that simply could not be overlooked. He

explained to those in attendance that there was a certain

young lady and her brother who were visiting Little Rock for

the holidays. Instead of squandering their time, the brother

and sister had come to the library where the older sister had

taught the younger brother to read. Grace blushed and Henry

became animated in his seat.

Mr. Valentine said it was truly an act of "Christmas

spirit" in the truest sense of the word. He then handed a

package to Grace and another to Henry.

Henry immediately tore open his package and he scream in delight as he yelled, "It's a 1957 Chevy model car, Grace! It even has glue," he said as he jumped up and down with joy. Then he looked at the janitor and the janitor winked.

The gesture between Henry and the janitor went unnoticed as she carefully opened her own gift. It was a new edition of all of Jane Austin's books, a collection which was contained in a beautifully-decorated box.

As Grace's eyes began to tear, Mrs. Jefferson went to her and gave her a hug saying, "Henry never would have learned without such a wonderful teacher, Grace."

Chapter Eighteen

As some of the staff began to clean up the party room,

Talia Jefferson led Grace and Henry back to her office to pick

up their backpacks and coats.

Henry seemed high as a kite with his gift securely held

by both hands. Grace didn't want to say anything to ruin the

day but, she was concerned about how they would get back to

the basement with so many people around. Some of the

guests seemed to want to linger and talk and she could not

figure out a good way to stay on without being noticed. She

thought perhaps she could go to the bathroom with Henry

and hide out there until everyone was gone. But then, she

realized the janitor would stay to clean up and there was no

way they would not be discovered.

As they entered Talia Jefferson's office, the librarian looked kindly at both of the children. They picked up their backpacks and began to put on their coats.

"Where will you go?" she asked, directing the question to Grace.

"Ah…," Grace replied with hesitation. "We'll be expected back at Nana's house. We can help with the last minute party preparations," she added.

Henry remained silent but Grace could see his anxiety creeping to the surface. He also understood they were in deep trouble. Even Grace no longer believed her own stories.

"I have another suggestion," Talia Jefferson said. Smiling at both children, she said, "Why don't you both sit down on that sofa for a minute."

The children did not fight the suggestion. It was almost as if the fight that had sustained them for years was waning and they were becoming defenseless.

"Let me tell you a story," the kindly librarian said.

JOURNEY

"Once upon a time, there was a small brother and his big sister," she began. And at that moment, Grace Elizabeth Gillian and Henry James Gillian both understood their lives were immediately and forever changed.

The librarian told the children she understood that their mother needed help and that she also understood the children were alone and staying in the library. She told Grace she had never before been so touched by Grace's ability to care for herself and her brother. She told Henry she was so proud of the dignified manner in which he had asked Santa to keep his mother and his sister safe from harm. In return, he wanted nothing for Christmas.

As the children listened intently to the unfolding of the story in which they had the lead roles, Henry's eyes lit up and he asked, "Is your janitor Mr. Winters a Santa's helper?" The librarian's eyes glistened as she told Henry how Santa had become suspicious when Henry said his sister would like books for Christmas and that they were spending their holiday break at the library. Santa had then approached the very librarian who was telling the story to the children.

When Santa discovered that Grace and Henry were at the library every day, he thought to check out the basement when they were out. He found a pair of Henry's underwear on one of the arms of the *octopus* boiler and felt he had enough evidence to confirm that the children were staying at the library after hours.

When Henry turned to his sister with a look of consternation on his face, Grace smiled and put her hand around her brother's shoulders. "Henry has always known just the right time to ask for help," Grace said.

The unfolding of the fairytale continued as the librarian told how she had called social services that very morning and due to the holiday season, the case worker that would now be assigned to Grace and Henry had eagerly agreed that Talia Jefferson and her husband would take in Grace and Henry for the balance of the holiday break. A decision would then be made as to a suitable placement should their mother not be located.

The librarian then told of how she and her husband had already agreed to take the required course to become foster parents so that Henry and Grace could remain in a stable home for as long as necessary. Tears rolled down the face of Henry Gillian and his sister reached out and stroked her brother's face.

And then, the sister asked if it was true that she and her brother would not be separated and the librarian answered that they would have to fight her all the way to Hell and back to do that.

After the story was told, the librarian took the children to the front of the library and got out her keys to lock the door. Grace said, "Just a minute; I forgot something." She ran down to the basement and retrieved the chicken drumsticks and then scampered up the stairs and joined the librarian and her brother as they went outside, each holding the librarian's hand.

The journey to their new home was short. When they entered the Jefferson house, Mr. Jefferson was there to greet them with a hearty smile. The children were surprised to discover that Mr. Jefferson was a black man. They were even more surprised to find that Mrs. Jefferson had passed as white for years.

"I'd never have gotten that job as a black woman," she explained.

■■

The journey to the Jefferson house was only the beginning of a longer journey that would carry Grace and Henry Gillian to adulthood, cloaked in a family atmosphere filled with abundant love and heartfelt appreciation.

LuAnn Gillian was eventually located in a halfway house in Baton Rouge, Louisiana. She had gone there after having been first admitted to a hospital for withdrawal from alcohol. It would be years before she would see her children. And when that occurred, they would all talk as friends. Lou Ann had relinquished all parental rights to Grace and Henry after her third relapse. LuAnn's final act of love for the children was to allow them to have a family of their own.

Other Books by Dr. Pirnot
As I Am
Just a Common Lady
The Learners of Owamboland
Keeper of the Lullabies

Children's Books: **Middle Grade Readers:**

A Colorful Day   Peter, the Pole and the Knob
Just Hanging Out   The Above All Others Principle
Night Traveler   Potsie and the Apparition of
Brave
                                     Wolf
Sam's Perfect Plan   Morgan and Clive
The Blue Penguin   The Days and Nights of Crighton
                                     Immanuel

The Colors of Myself
The Door in the Floor
Rainbows Are the Best
Please Be My Hands

**To contact Dr. Pirnot or to order books,
go to:**
www.drpirnotbooks.com

18901148R00094

Made in the USA
Lexington, KY
28 November 2012